THE CITY IN THE SAHARA

Jules Verne   *Frontispiece by John Betancourt*

The City in the Sahara

Part Two of
The Barsac Mission

by
JULES VERNE

★

Translated from the French by
I.O. Evans

Introductions by
I.O. Evans *and* Darrell Schweitzer

WILDSIDE PRESS

First published 1960 by Arco Publications
Second Impression November 1960
© *Arco Publications 1960*

First published under the title
L'Étonnante Aventure de la Mission Barsac

MEET JULES VERNE

Jules Verne (1828-1905) was a French writer and one of the founding fathers of science fiction, although, surprisingly, his only novel about the future, *Paris in the 21ˢᵗ Century* (1863) was rejected in his lifetime and not actually published until 1994. He was trained in law and briefly worked as a stockbroker, but soon committed himself to literature. After a brief start with short stories and plays he came to specialize in "Voyages Extraordinaires," which combined adventure and travel writing with his enthusiasm for scientific discovery and new technology. His best-known works include *A Journey to the Center of the Earth* (1864), *From the Earth to the* Moon (1865), Twenty *Thousand Leagues under the Sea* (1870), *Around the World in Eighty Days* (1872), and *The Mysterious Island* (1875). All of these have been filmed repeatedly, with great success.

Not all of Verne's novels, or even all the "Voyages" contain fantastic elements. Indeed, one of his most popular novels has always been *Michael Strogoff* (1876) is an adventure story, set in Russia, and there is nothing quite fantastic in *Around the World in Eighty Days*, although the conclusion hinges on a scientific point, that the hero gained a day by crossing the International Date Line in an easterly direction. It also inspired a science fictional sequel, *The Other Log of Phineas Fogg* by Philip Jose Farmer (1973). Verne transported his readers to places they had never been, into situations few had imagined, although his stories were set in his own time, in hidden corners of the world. What makes him more than an adventure writer, of course, is the speculative elements: Captain Nemo's submarine, lunar flight, the massive flying machine (an aerial battleship) in *Robur the Conqueror* (1886) and *Master of the World* (1904). The lesser-known *The Begum's Fortune* (1879) involves an attempt to create two "utopian" communities (in the Cascades, in Oregon, which seemed remote enough to French readers of Verne's time), one of them run by a mad German militarist who develops super-weapons. If you consider the repeating motif here, of a super-scientist outcast/

misanthrope with an exotic, secret base, a small army of devoted followers, and super-scientific weapons or other technology far in advance of the rest of the world, one might consider that, for all Captain Nemo is somewhat sympathetic and Robur proposes to subdue the world to put an end to war, Verne came very close to inventing the James Bond villain. All he needed was a secret-agent hero to bring such reigns of terror to an end.

Verne's work was enormously influential. M.P. Shiel's *The Lord of the Sea* (1901), for example, would not possibly have existed without the example of Verne's Robur and Nemo. The novels of George Griffith, *The Angel of the Revolution* (1893) and any of a number of other late Victorian stories about aerial warfare owe much to *Robur the Conqueror.* Verne was the predecessor of modern "hard" science fiction, since he insisted that what happened in his stories be scientifically plausible. He was reported to have sneered at the anti-gravity metal, "cavorite," used to propel a spaceship in H.G. Wells' *The First Men in the Moon* (1901), "Let him produce it." Wells might have asked how Captain Nemo's *Nautilus* is powered. Like most hard-sf writers, Verne was capable of stretching things a bit when a good story required it, and he was, above all else, a superb storyteller.

His reputation has always been high in France and in much of the rest of Europe, if ill-served in the English-speaking world by bad 19th century translations, and the tendency to relegate his books to the Boys Adventure category, which tends to overlook the richness of his ideas and his frequently caustic satire. He has been the subject of renewed critical attention in recent years, and remains a seminal figure.

—Darrell Schweitzer
Philadelphia, Pennsylvania

INTRODUCTION

BOOK I of Jules Verne's posthumous story, *L'Étonnante Aventure de la Mission Barsac,* published in this series under the title *Into the Niger Bend,* described the vicissitudes of the Barsac Mission, sent out at the beginning of the Nineteenth Century to ascertain whether the negroes of French West Africa were qualified to become voters and citizens. After being threatened and impeded, robbed of its armed escort and of its native porters, its members were pounced on in mysterious circumstances, pinioned, and threatened with death.

Accompanying the Mission was a young English girl, Jane Blazon, passing under the pseudonym of Jane Mornas. With her elderly nephew, Agénor de St. Bérain, she had undertaken the journey to clear the name of her brother, George Blazon, accused of having turned traitor and led the native troops he commanded in murderous attacks on the negroes. In his grave at Koubo she found evidence of his innocence; instead of having been shot down by a punitive expedition, as was alleged, he had been deliberately murdered from behind by some unknown assassin, who was presumably guilty of the Blazon column's atrocities.

By taking this news to her father, Lord Blazon of Glenor, Jane hoped to restore the old man's peace of mind, shattered by this stain on the family honour, but the kidnapping of the Mission had precluded this. Meantime, unknown to her, Lewis Blazon, also her brother, had vanished after a bank robbery in which he was suspected of complicity.

The events which followed the kidnapping of the Barsac Mission and of Jane Blazon are described in the present volume. They illustrate Jules Verne's inventive genius as well as his ability to keep abreast of the latest scientific and technical advances and to weave them into his narrative. Unpublished until after his death in 1905, the story incorporates inventions made towards the end of his life, notably that of wireless telegraphy. It shows that he shared in the contemporary belief, not justified by events, that liquid air was the motive power of the future. But it also illustrates his remarkable powers of foresight in his description of rocket-propelled missiles, aircraft with a vertical take-off and automatic stabilizers, and the attempt to control the weather by inducing passing clouds to discharge themselves in rain.

He was plainly aware of early experiments with airplanes, and may have known of the achievements of the Wright Brothers. Yet Verne himself had pinned his faith not to the airplane but to the helicopter.[1] An attempt to take advantage of both types may have produced the aircraft which he called *Planeurs*—though their nature is more graphically expressed by the term I have substituted.

As in Book I the names of some of the characters have been altered to avoid a possible clash with those of actual people. But the titles of this mysterious city, of its varied inhabitants, and of its ruler, are those given by the author himself.

In my introduction to Book I, I put forward a possible reason why so remarkable a work does not seem to have been hitherto translated into English. The continuation of the narrative suggests another, that at the time it seemed too far-fetched even for Jules Verne.

In those orderly days the notion of a super-scientific community ruled by criminals seemed beyond the bounds of possibility. We have seen such communities—not mere cities but nations—compared to which the City in the Sahara seems almost tame.

Here Verne's prophetic gifts misled him only by falling short of the truth. Yet the story remains an example of the symbolism which he could use so effectively. His Blackland typifies much in our civilization, its triumphs of technology and its material advances compared with its backwardness—indeed with its retrogression—in moral and spiritual develop-

[1]See, for example, his account of its advantages over other types of aircraft in his story, *The Clipper of the Clouds*.

ment, the threat implicit in its very nature that the misuse of its mighty powers will end in its own destruction.

Nevertheless his strong religious faith forbade Verne to despair of humanity. The stronghold of material progress may be shattered, but from its ruins come the decent people, the gentle and humble of heart, preserved—humanly speaking—by their idealism, their sense of duty, their moral integrity, and their mutual faith.

I.O.E.

CHAPTER I

BLACKLAND

AT THE beginning of the century even the most accurate and recent of maps represented the Sahara, that immense stretch of nearly 300,000 square miles, only by a blank space. When the Mission led by the Deputy Barsac underwent the trials described in the first part of this narrative, nobody had crossed it, nobody had entered it. It was completely unknown.

At that time, the strangest legends circulated about that unexplored region. Sometimes, so the natives said, they had seen immense black birds with outspread wings and fiery eyes flying towards or into these arid plains. Sometimes a horde of great red devils, mounted on plunging horses whose nostrils emitted flames, had suddenly emerged from that mysterious land. These uncanny horsemen galloped into the towns, slaying, massacring all whom they found in their way, then returning to the desert, and carrying across their saddles men, women, and children who never returned.

Who were these miscreants who destroyed the villages, pillaged the huts, looted the miserable treasures of the poor negroes, and disappeared, leaving behind them ruin, despair and death? Nobody knew. Nobody had tried to find out. Who, indeed, would dare to follow enemies believed to be endowed with supernatural powers, the fierce deities of the desert?

Such were the rumours which spread along the Niger, and as far as a hundred miles from its bank.

If, more daring than these timid negroes, someone had ventured into the desert, and if this hero had reached, at the cost of a journey of over 150 miles, a point 1° 40′ east and 15° 50′ north, he would have reaped the reward of his courage. He would have seen something that nobody had ever seen before, neither the explorers nor the caravans : a city.

Yes, a town, a real town, which did not appear on any

12   THE CITY OF THE SAHARATHE CITY OF THE SAHARA

map, and of which nobody suspected the existence, although its total population, not counting children, was not less than 6,808.

If the hypothetical traveller had asked the name of the town, and if one of its inhabitants had been willing to tell him, he would perhaps have said in French *"Le nom de cette ville est Terre-noire":* but he would be just as likely to reply in Italian *"Questa città è Terra Nera";* in Bambara, *"Ni doug-ouba ntocko a bé Bankou Fing";* in Portuguese, *"Hista ciudad e Terranegra";* in Spanish, *"Esta ciudad es Tierranegra."* But no matter in what the language, all the answers would have meant : "The name of this city is Blackland."

The information might even be given in Latin : *"Ista urbs Terra Nigra est."* The enquirer would simply be dealing with Josias Eberly, a one-time professor who, having found in Blackland no use for his erudition, had opened a shop and become, as his sign somewhat unidiomatically indicated, "Josias Eberly, Druggist, Products for Dye."

Every language was spoken in this new Tower of Babel, whose population, when the Barsac Mission collapsed near Koubo, comprised, apart from 5,778 negroes and negresses, 1,030 whites. Though these had come from all parts of the world, most of them had one thing in common; escaped from the hulks or the prison, they were adventurers capable of anything except the right, outcasts ready for the worst jobs. However, just as in that motley crowd representatives of the English race predominated, so the English language took precedence. It was in English that the Chief published his proclamations and the local government, so far as there was a local government, its decrees; and the town's official journal was *The Blackland Thunderbolt.*

Very remarkable that journal, as can be judged from extracts from several issues :

"To-day John Andrew hanged the negro Koromoko, who had forgotten to bring him his after-lunch pipe."

"To-morrow evening, at six, ten heliplanes will set out for Kourkoussou and Bidi, with ten Merry Fellows commanded by Colonel Hiram Herbert. Total raid on these two villages, which we haven't visited for three years; return the same night."

"We have learned that a French Mission, directed by a Deputy called Barsac, is soon to set out from Konakry. This Mission had, it appears, the intention of reaching the Niger by way of Sikasso and Ouaghadougou. We have taken precautions. Twenty of the Black Guard and two Merry Fellows will keep in touch with them continually. Captain Edward Rufus will join them at some convenient time. Rufus who, as we know, is a deserter from the Colonial Infantry, will play, under the name of Lacour, the role of a French lieutenant, and will take advantage of his command of that nation's military usages, so as to check, somehow or other, the said Barsac, making certain that he does not reach the Niger."

"To-day, on the Garden Bridge, as the result of a discussion, Counsellor Ehle Willis found himself under the necessity of putting some bullets into the head of Merry Fellow Constantin Bernard. The latter fell into the Red River, where, borne down by the abnormal weight of his skull, so recently filled with lead, he was drowned. A session was at once opened to replace the deceased. It was Gilman Ely who received this honour, having seventeen sentences inflicted by the courts of France, England and Germany, and achieved the total of 29 years in prison and 35 years in the hulks. Gilman Ely will thus be transferred from the Civil Body to the Merry Fellows. Our best wishes go with him."

It will be seen that the personages in question were designated only by their forenames. This was the custom in Blackland, where every new arrival lost his family name, which was known only to the Chief. Alone among the white inhabitants, apart from a special group to be described later, that Chief was known in the ordinary way. Even then his name must have been a nickname, at once terrible and sinister. He was called Harry Killer.

Ten years before the remains of the Barsac Mission had been rounded up as explained in part I of this book, Harry Killer, coming from nobody knows where with several others of the same kidney, had reached that part of the desert where Blackland was to rise. There he had pitched his tent and said "The town will be here." And Blackland had arisen from the sand as though by enchantment.

It was a remarkable place. On level ground, on the right bank of the Tafasasset Oued, a gully dry until the decree of Harry Killer filled it with water, it was built in a precise semi-circle, measuring exactly 1200 yards from north-east to south-west parallel to the stream and 600 yards from north-west to south-east. Its surface thus comprised over a hundred acres and was divided into three unequal sections, bounded by unscaleable semi-circular walls of compressed clay, over thirty feet high and almost as thick at their base.

Nearest the banks of the stream, renamed the Red River by Harry Killer, the first section had a radius of two hundred and fifty yards. A boulevard a hundred yards wide extended from the points where it joined the second section along the river bank as far as the third. This increased its surface to about thirty-five acres.

In the first section lived the aristocracy of Blackland; these were called, by way of antithesis, the Merry Fellows. Except for a few meant for higher destiny, Harry Killer's original companions had been the embryo of this corps. Around this nucleus had soon gathered a horde of bandits, escaped from prison or the hulks, to whom Killer had promised full satisfaction of their detestable instincts. Soon the Merry Fellows had grown to number 566, a total not to be exceeded on any pretext.

Their functions were numerous. Organized on military lines,

with a colonel, five captains, ten lieutenants and fifty sergeants, respectively commanding five hundred, one hundred, fifty, and ten men, they formed the army of Blackland and levied war. A war devoid of honour, moreover, a war of loot, consisting only of pillaging the wretched villages and of massacring or enslaving all their inhabitants. The Merry Fellows also acted as the police of the town; by blows—except when they used their revolvers—they controlled the slaves who performed the agricultural and other work. But above all they formed the Chief's body-guard and obeyed his orders blindly.

The town's third section, the most distant from the centre, formed a semi-circular arc, about six hundred yards long and fifty wide. Its two extremities abutted on the first section and on the Red River, and it followed the circuit of the town, between its outer boundary, and that of the second section, where the slaves were parked.

In this third section there lived, under the general name of the Civil Body, the whites not permitted in the first. While waiting for a place to become vacant in this—which did not take very long, for the brutal customs of Blackland caused frequent deaths—they spent their time in the Civil Body, which could thus be considered as a purgatory whose paradise would be the Merry Fellows.

To subsist until then, for only the Merry Fellows were supported by the Chief and the town's communal activities, they went in for trade. Their section was thus the commercial quarter of the town, and it was there that the Merry Fellows could buy countless products, including the most luxurious. These the merchants bought from the Chief, who gained them either as plunder or else, as regards articles of European origin, by methods known only to himself and his immediate entourage.

This third section comprised 246 inhabitants, including 45 white women, who were worth no more than their male fellow-citizens of the same colour.

Between the first and the third section was the second, with a surface of about 63 acres. This was the slaves' quarter, their number then being 5,778, of which 4,196 were men and 1,582 women. It was there, almost without exception, that they dwelt. There were their huts. There they spent their wretched lives.

Each morning the four doors in its wall opened, and, driven by Merry Fellows armed with bludgeons and guns, those of the negroes who were not busied with the town's upkeep went, by brigades, to the agricultural work. In the evening the miserable herd returned in the same manner, and the heavy doors closed until the next day. There was no exit to the outer world. On one side the Merry Fellows, on the other the Civil Body. On all sides beings equally bloodthirsty and equally fierce.

Many of these wretches died, either from the privations they suffered, or under the blows of their guardians too often transformed into murderers. This was a trifling misfortune. Another raid would soon fill the gaps, and other martyrs would replace those freed by death.

But these districts on the right bank did not form the whole of Blackland. On the left bank of the Red River the ground rose abruptly to form a hill about fifty yards high. Here the outer wall extended, marking out a rectangle twelve hundred yards along the riverside and three hundred yards from its banks. This second town, scarcely smaller than the first, for it covered about seventy acres, was itself divided into two equal parts by a high transverse wall.

One of these halves, on the north-east slope of the hill, had been converted into the Fortress Garden, a public park communicating at its northern end, by means of the Garden Bridge, with the sections occupied by the Merry Fellows and the Civil Body. The other half, placed on the summit, contained the vital organs of the city.

In the northern corner, beside the public garden, rose a huge quadrangular construction, surrounded by flanking walls; its north-west face towered over the Red River from a height

of about ninety feet. Usually called the Palace, this was the
home of Harry Killer and nine of his companions, promoted
to the rank of Counsellors. Strange Counsellors, the habitual
accomplices in their Chief's crimes. Strange Counsellors, whose
chief function was the immediate execution of the orders of a
master who was inaccessible and almost always invisible, and
from whose sentences there was no appeal.

Another bridge, barred by a solid grille during the night,
the Castle Bridge, connected the seat of government with the
right bank.

To the Palace were annexed two barracks. One was assigned
to a dozen slaves who acted as servants, and also to fifty
negroes, chosen from those who seemed to have the fiercest
natural instincts, and who formed the Black Guard. In the
other lived forty whites selected on the same principle; to these
was confided the use of the flying machines spoken of in Blackland as heliplanes.

A wonderful invention of a brain of genius, these heliplanes
were powerful machines, able to travel without refuelling up
to three thousand miles at an average speed of two hundred
and fifty miles an hour. To these heliplanes the pirates of
Blackland owed the gift of ubiquity which they seemed to
possess, enabling them to vanish as soon as a crime was committed. On these heliplanes the despotic power of Harry Killer
chiefly rested.

It was indeed by terror that he governed the unknown
empire of which Blackland was the capital, by terror that he
had established and maintained his authority. Nevertheless
the autocrat had not failed to foresee a revolt of his subjects,
black or white. Prudently he had so placed the Palace that it
dominated and threatened with its guns the town, the garden,
and the barracks. Any revolt would be the signal for a
massacre, from which there would be no escape. The desert
formed an insuperable barrier, and anyone who entered that
robber's lair must forever renounce all hope of coming out.

For the rest, Blackland was kept perfectly clean, and well

maintained, and was provided with every possible commodity. Not a house of the Merry Fellows or the Civil Body which did not have its own telephone. Not a street, not a house— not even a hut in the slaves' quarters—which did not enjoy water from the mains, and which was not lighted by electricity.

Around the city, founded ten years before in sheer desert, the marvels were greater still. Though the sea of sand still surrounded it, this did not now begin for several miles from its wall. In the immediate vicinity of the city, on a tract so great that its limits were hidden beyond the horizon, the desert had given place to fields cultivated by the most efficient methods; here were grown, with ever-increasing success, all the vegetables of Africa and Europe.

Such was the work of Harry Killer, a work which would have been admirable if its basis and purpose had not been crime. But how had he performed it? How had he fertilized these arid and desiccated plains? Water is the one element indispensable to all plant and animal life, for man to live, for the earth to bring forth. How had Harry Killer contrived to bestow it upon this region where whole years had elapsed without a single drop of rain? Was he endowed with a magical power by which he alone could achieve such miracles?

No, Harry Killer possessed no supernatural power; left to his own devices he could never have accomplished such marvels. But Harry Killer was not alone. The Palace, where he lived with those whom he had the effrontery to call his Counsellors, the barracks of the Black Guard, and the heliplane sheds, together occupied only a small part of the last section of Blackland. In the midst of the great open space there were other erections, or rather there was another town contained within the first; its different buildings, with their yards and inner gardens, themselves covered nearly twenty acres. Before the Palace rose the Factory.

The Factory was an independent and autonomous city on which the Chief had lavished wealth, which he respected, which, without admitting it to himself, he even feared a little.

If he had devised the town, it was the Factory which had
created it, which had equipped it not only with all modern
amenities but with astonishing inventions which Europe was
not to know until years later.

The Factory had a soul and a body. The soul was its Director. The body comprised about a hundred or so workmen
belonging to different nationalities but mostly to France and
England, chosen from among the foremost in their respective
professions, and transported over a bridge of gold. Each of
them received a ministerial salary, and in return he had to
submit to the inflexible rule of Blackland.

Almost the whole of this technical body consisted of workmen, of whom skilled mechanics formed the majority. Several
were married, so that the Factory contained twenty-seven
women, with a few children.

This population of honest workers, who contrasted so
strangely with the town's other inhabitants, all lived in the
Factory, and from this they were strictly forbidden ever to
emerge. Even if they had wanted to, they could not have done
so, a careful watch being kept up day and night by the Black
Guard and the Merry Fellows. But they had been warned of
this when they were engaged, and not one of them felt any
temptation to break this rule. In return for the high salary
offered them, they had to consider themselves as withdrawn
from the world throughout the time they would spend at
Blackland. Not only might they never leave the Factory, they
could neither write to anyone nor receive any letter from outside.

Though many had recoiled at the stringency of such conditions, several had let themselves be tempted by increases in
the promised salary. What had they to lose, after all, when
they were poor and had to struggle to earn their daily bread?
The chance of wealth was well worth the disadvantage of
facing the unknown; and after all, they reassured themselves,
they risked nothing except a little adventure.

The contract signed, it was at once carried out. The new

employee embarked on an assigned vessel and this took him to
one of the Bissago Islands, an archipelago off the coast of
Portuguese Guinea, where he was landed. There he had to
agree to be blindfolded, and one of the heliplanes, for which
a shelter had been made at a deserted spot on the shore, took
him in less than six hours to Blackland, about fourteen hundred miles away as the crow flies. The heliplane landed in the
Esplanade between the Palace and the Factory, and the workman, freed from his bandage, entered the latter never to
emerge until the time came to terminate his contract and to
return to his native land.

On this point, indeed, the contract arranged for the employee to be repatriated. If he were a prisoner so long as he
remained in Blackland, he had the option at any time of
leaving the town for ever. Then another heliplane would take
him from the Esplanade and fly him to the Bissago Islands,
where he would find a steamer to take him to Europe.

Such, at any rate, was the assurance given to the workmen
who wished to leave. What their comrades in the Factory did
not know, however, was that those who left in this way never
arrived at their destination, that their bones were bleaching
somewhere in the desert, that their salaries were invariably
reclaimed by those who paid them. Thus the city's cash-box
never became empty, thus was kept secret the existence of
Blackland, and thus the empire of Harry Killer remained unknown.

None the less these departures were rare. Utterly unable to
know, or even to suspect, the life lived by the town's inhabitants, on which they had not a vestige of information, it was
only exceptionally that the workmen asked to leave their city.
Among them lived nine black slaves of both sexes, prisoners
like themselves, who helped the women with their domestic
work. The workpeople were, in short, happier than they had
been in their native land, engaged in work so congenial that
sometimes they would spontaneously continue it far into the
night.

The workmen had only one chief, their Director, a French-man called Marcel Camaret, whom they looked upon almost as a god.

Alone among the Factory's inhabitants, Marcel Camaret was free to come and go at will, both about the streets and about the country round Blackland. Although he was not slow to use his freedom and to walk about wrapped in thought, it should not be inferred that he was better informed than the personnel under him regarding the peculiar habits of the town, of which he did not so much as know the name.

One day a workman asked him what it was. Camaret reflected deeply for a moment; then, to the great astonishment of his employee, he replied: "Well, really, I don't know either."

Never until then had he thought of wondering about such a detail. What's more, after the question had been put to him he never thought of it again.

He was a strange person, this Marcel Camaret.

He seemed about forty years old. Medium in height, with straight shoulders and flat-chested, his scanty dull-blond hair gave him an aspect of frail delicacy. His gestures were slight, his calm imperturbable, and he spoke, with a childlike timidity, in a weak gentle voice which, whatever the circumstances, never rose to tones of anger, or even of impatience. He always kept his head bent towards his left shoulder as though he felt it too heavy, and his face, which was pale and insipid, with a delicate sickly look, possessed only one beauty : attractive blue eyes which suggested lofty thoughts.

A careful observer would have noticed something else in those splendid eyes. At certain moments a vague troubled gleam passed over them, and for an instant they took on a lost look. Anyone who had surprised that look would not have failed to suspect that Marcel Camaret was insane, and perhaps after all he would not have been far wrong. Is it not a very small distance, indeed, between super-intelligence and insanity? Does not genius border on madness?

In spite of his timidity, his bodily weakness and his gentleness, Marcel Camaret was endowed with boundless energy. The greatest misfortunes, the most imminent dangers, the most cruel privations, left him unmoved. This was because he did not know about them. His clear blue eyes were always turned inwards and saw nothing of what happened around him. He lived beyond time, in a fantastic world peopled with wild imaginations. He thought. He thought deeply, he thought exclusively and always. Marcel Camaret was nothing but a thinking machine, a machine mighty, inoffensive and terrible.

So absent-minded that he could have given points to St. Bérain; he was so 'foreign' to all that constitutes material life he had more than once tumbled into the Red River, thinking he was crossing a bridge. His servant, whose monkey-like appearance had earned him the name of Jacko, could not make him take his meals at regular hours. Marcel Camaret ate when he felt hungry, and slept when he felt sleepy, which was as likely to be noon as at midnight.

Ten years earlier, circumstances had brought him into the path of Harry Killer. A remarkable device able to produce rain was then among his imaginings. He did not hesitate to describe his dreams to anyone who would listen to them, and Harry Killer, with some others, had heard of this invention while it was still a mere theory. But, while the others only laughed at such madness, Harry Killer had taken it seriously, so much so that he had made it the basis of his schemes.

If Harry Killer was a bandit, he was at least a bandit with a wide outlook, and at least he had the merit of understanding how he might make use of an unrecognized genius. Chance having placed Camaret in his power, he had dazzled the scientist's eyes with the realization of his dreams. Taking him to the desert-spot where Blackland was to rise, he had said : "Make the promised rain fall here!" And the rain had obediently begun to fall.

Since then Camaret had lived in a perpetual fever. All his visions had materialized one by one. After the rain-machine, his brain had produced a hundred other inventions from which Harry Killer had profited, without their inventor's ever troubling about how they were used.

Though no inventor can be held responsible for the evil of which he was the indirect cause, whoever invented the revolver must have realized that such a weapon could and must slay, and it was clearly with that end in mind that he had thought of it.

Such was not true of Marcel Camaret. If it had ever occurred to him to design a cannon whose range would be greater and whose projectile heavier than ever before, he would gladly have calculated the proportions of the weapon, the weight and design of the shell and the quantity of the explosive, without having seen in this anything more than a curiosity of ballistics. He would have been greatly surprised to learn that the child of his brain could be used for destruction.

Harry Killer had asked for rain, and Camaret had caused it; Harry Killer had asked for agricultural instruments, and Camaret had produced ploughs, sowing-machines, weeding-machines, reapers, threshers, which ploughed, sowed, weeded, reaped, threshed, without needing a separate motor; Harry Killer had asked for flying-machines, and Camaret had given him the heliplanes, able to travel three thousand miles with meteoric speed.

As for the use which his companion made of these inventions, Marcel Camaret had never even thought of asking. A creature of abstract thought, he had seen them only as pure problems without worrying either about their practical application or about the origin of the materials he was given. Though he had been present without realizing it at the birth of Blackland and at the progressive substitution of fertile land for the desert, he had never had the remotest wish to know the methods by which Harry Killer had equipped him with the first instruments and machines which enabled the Factory to make the others.

Marcel Camaret had first asked, as though it were the simplest thing in the world, for a factory to be built, and at once hundreds of negroes had built it. He had then asked for such-and-such a machine-tool, for dynamos and a steam-engine, and, sometimes almost at once, sometimes months later, the machine-tools, the dynamos, and the engine had arrived as though by miracle in the desert.

He had asked for workmen, and, one after another, the workmen had come in the numbers he desired. How had such marvels been accomplished? Marcel Camaret did not worry about that. He had asked for them, he had got them. To him, nothing seemed simpler.

Nor had he ever dreamed of working out the amount of capital absorbed in realizing his dreams, and never had he asked the very natural question : "Where's the money coming from?"

At the moment when this narrative began, all was as usual in Blackland. The Factory personnel were busy at work; some of the Merry Fellows were supervising the negroes at the agricultural toil necessitated by the approach of the rainy season, the others as usual giving themselves up to the grossest pleasures; and the Civil Body was occupied a little vaguely in its highly restricted and irregular trade.

About eleven in the morning, Harry Killer was alone in his private room. He was thinking deeply, and to judge by his expression his thoughts cannot have been pleasant.

The telephone bell rang.

"Listening !" he said, as he grasped the receiver.

"West, seventeen degrees south, ten heliplanes in sight," the telephone announced.

"Coming up !" said Harry Killer, replacing the apparatus.

In a few seconds he had reached the Palace roof, above which rose a tower about thirty feet high; on to this he climbed. On the platform was the Merry Fellow who had warned him.

"There," he said, indicating a direction.

Harry Killer turned his telescope that way.

"That's them," he said, after a short examination.

"Call the Counsellors," he added. "I'm going down."

While the Merry Fellow was telephoning the various members of the Council, Harry Killer quickly descended to the Esplanade between the Factory and the Palace. There the nine Counsellors came one by one to join him. Their eyes lifted skywards, they waited.

The delay was short. The heliplanes seemed to get larger as they approached. A few minutes later they landed gently on the Esplanade.

The eyes of Harry Killer gleamed with delight. If four of the heliplanes contained only their respective pilots, the other six each carried two passengers : a man of the Black Guard and a prisoner firmly bound and with the head muffled in a hood.

The six prisoners were released from their bonds. When their dazzled eyes had grown used to the daylight they looked round them in surprise. They found themselves in a wide open space surrounded on all sides by unscaleable walls. A few paces away were the strange contrivances which had carried them through the air. Before them the vast bulk of the Palace was surmounted by its tower, and thirty negroes of the Black Guard formed a compact group.

Behind them, more than a hundred yards away, was a wall two hundred and fifty yards long with neither door nor window, above which appeared a tall factory chimney and a frail-looking metallic pylon which rose higher still, but whose purpose they did not know. Where were they? What was this fortress not shown on any of the maps of Africa which they had studied so carefully and so long?

While they were asking themselves these questions, Harry Killer made a sign, and a brutal hand fell on the shoulder of each of the prisoners. Willy-nilly they entered the Palace, whose door swung open before them and closed itself after them.

Jane Blazon, St. Bérain, Barsac, Amédée Florence, Dr. Châtonnay and M. Poncin were in the power of Harry Killer, the dictator of Blackland, the unknown capital of an unknown empire.

CHAPTER II

WITH WINGS OUTSPREAD

(From the note-book of Amédée Florence)

25th March. It is now nearly twenty-four hours since we have been at. . . . But where in fact are we? If someone told me I was in the Moon, it wouldn't surprise me much, given the mode of travel whose charms we've just tasted. The truth is that I haven't the slightest idea.

Whatever the facts, I can quite accurately express myself as follows : It isn't twenty-four hours since we were made prisoner, and it was only this morning, after a night otherwise peaceful, that I felt strong enough to add these notes to my record, which I daresay was beginning to get a little sparse.

In spite of the lesson in aerial equestrianism which we've been forced to take, our general health is excellent, and we are all in good shape except that St. Bérain is more firmly nailed to his bed by a fierce lumbago than by a steel chain. The poor man, as stiff as a post, cannot make the slightest movement, and we have to feed him like a child. There's nothing surprising in that. What is surprising is that any of us can move, after yesterday's little outing. All that day I was in no condition to put two ideas together. Today things are a little better but not too good. Still let's try to collect our ideas and to sum things up.

Well, the day before yesterday we had turned in. We were tired out and we were sleeping the sleep of the just, when just before dawn we were awakened by an infernal din. It was the same roaring that had intrigued me three times before, but this time it was ever so much more intense. We opened our eyes but had to close them at once, for we were dazzled by blazing lights seemingly thrown from some distance above us.

We had not recovered from the din and the no less inexplicable brilliance when without warning some men threw themselves on us. We were hustled, thrown down, bound, gagged, and blinded by some sort of bag into which our heads and shoulders were crammed. All this in less time than it takes to write. There's nothing more to be said: it was a masterpiece.

In an instant I was trussed up like a sausage. On my ankles, on my knees, on my wrists which someone had carefully crossed behind my back, were bonds cutting into my flesh. It was lovely!

When I was beginning to realize this pleasant sensation, I heard a voice, in which I recognized the enchanting tones of Lieutenant Lacour saying harshly:

"Are you there, boys?"

Then almost at once, without giving the boys—charming boys, no doubt—time to reply, the same voice added even more roughly:

"The first to move will get a bullet in his head. Come on, you there, let's get going!"

No need to be a doctor of literature to realize that the second speech was meant for us. He's a good one, the ex-commandant of our escort! Move? It's easy to talk. No, I shall not move, and for a very good reason. But I listen.

At once someone answers the energetic lieutenant:

"Heruntersteigen können wir hier nicht. Es gibt zu viele Baüme."

Although I can scarcely understand the jargon, I bet this is German. M. Barsac, adept in that craggy language, has since told me that I'd won, and that it means: "We can't come down here, there's too many trees." That's quite likely.

Anyhow, I didn't understand it at the time. But what did strike me was that this Teutonic sentence had been shouted from a distance, I might even say from above.

Scarcely was it said when in the midst of the continual

din, a third voice added in the same tones, a howl: "It's necessary to take away your prisoners until the end of the trees."

Well, now it's English! Versed in the language of Shakespeare, I at once realized what this unidiomatic sentence—not I think, spoken by an Englishman—really means: we are to be taken beyond the copse. Then Lieutenant Lacour—I suppose—asks:

"Which way?"

"Towards Kourboussou," cries the stepson of perfidious Albion.

"How far?" asks the lieutenant.

"Circa venti chilometri," yells a fourth voice.

A latinist such as myself can easily guess that these three words are Italian and mean about twenty kilometers. Are we in the land of the linguists then, or, at least, in the backwoods of Babel?

However this may be, Lieutenant Lacour replies:

"All right, I'll set off at dawn," and nobody takes any more notice of me. I stay where I am, flat on my back, bound, seeing nothing, hardly able to breathe, in the not over comfortable cowl into which I've been stuffed.

At the lieutenant's reply, the roaring at once doubles its volume, only to decrease in strength and at last die away. In a few minutes it can no longer be heard.

Whatever makes that strange uproar? Of course, my gag keeps me from getting into touch with the others, and it is only to myself that I put that question—to which, naturally, there comes no reply.

Time passes. After an hour or more two men grab hold of me, one by the feet and the other by the shoulders, swing me to and fro for a moment and then throw me like a sack of corn across a saddle, with the pommel digging me in the back, on a horse which sets off at a gallop.

Never had I thought, even in my most fantastic dreams, that I should one day play the part of Mazeppa in the heart of Africa, and I ask you to believe that thinking about the prowess of that Cossack has never kept me awake.[1]

I was wondering if I should end by getting out of it as he did, and if it would be my fate to become hetman of the Bambaras when a half-drunken voice, coming from a throat which must have been rinsed with paraffin, said in a way to make the flesh creep :

"Take care, old bloody toad! If you budge, this revolver shall hinder you to begin again."

That's twice that I've been given the same advice, always in the same barbarous English and with the same exquisite politeness. This is luxury!

Around me there's the sound of furious galloping, and sometimes I can hear dull groans; my companions, no doubt —they must be as bady off as I am. Because I'm very badly off, indeed! I'm stifling, and the blood's running to my head. I feel it's going to burst, my poor head which hangs so piteously over the right flank of the horse, while at every stride my feet are beating a tattoo against its left flank.

After about an hour of this mad rush, the cavalcade suddenly halts. I'm lifted from the horse, or rather I'm thrown to earth like a bundle of old rags. A few seconds pass, then faintly enough, for I'm three parts dead, I can hear an exchange of words :

"She is died !"

"No Ell'è solamenta svenita." ("No, she's only fainted.")

"Unwrap her," orders, in French, the voice which I attribute to Lieutenant Lacour, "and unwrap the doctor as well."

"This woman. . . . Is Miss Blazon in danger?"

I feel myself released from the sack and gag which kept me from seeing and breathing. Do my executioners fancy, by any

---

[1]A stirring poem, *Mazeppa's Ride,* describes the emotions of Ivan Stepanovitch Mazeppa, an Ukrainian, when, having offended a nobleman, he was bound to the back of a fiery untamed steed which was then turned loose to gallop over the Steppes. Mazeppa was however rescued by the Cossacks and rose to be their hetman (Military commander)—I.O.E.

chance, that under these somewhat unattractive toilet articles
they're going to find Dr. Châtonnay? Yes, that's just why
they busied themselves with my humble person, for as soon as
they realized their mistake :

"That isn't him. Get the other!" says the chief, who as I
suspected is indeed Lieutenant Lacour.

I look at him, and I silently utter the most frightful curses.
To think I took him for a French officer! . . . Admittedly, I
can truthfully say, on my word of honour, that I had suspected
the trick from the outset. But I had only suspected it, and not
unmasked the bandit under his borrowed plumes. That, as I
explained, I've paid for with my head, and it drives me mad.
Oh, the scum! . . . If ever I get hold of him!

Just then someone comes up and speaks to him, so I hear
his real name : Captain Edward Rufus. Captain, indeed! He
could be a general, and I shouldn't think any the better of
him.

While he's talking, Captain Rufus has given up paying
attention to me. I take the opportunity of breathing. It is
time. A little more, and I should have been asphyxiated. That
must be obvious, and I seem to have turned purple, for the
captain, having thrown a glance at me, gives an order which
I cannot understand. I'm at once searched. They take my
weapons, and my money, but they leave my note-book. These
brutes don't realize the value of copy signed "Amédée Florence." Good heavens, what ignorant thieves I'm dealing
with!

But the stupid brutes untie my arms and legs, and I can
move. I take advantage of this without hesitation, and examine
my surroundings.

What first attracts my attention are ten . . . what? . . . ten
. . . machines, ten, hum! things . . . systems . . . ten objects,
in short, for devil take me if I can make out what they're for,
and they look like nothing I've ever seen.

Imagine a fairly broad platform supported by two large
skates turned up at one end. From this platform rises a pylon

of trellis four by five meters high; half-way up there's a screw of two blades and at its top two. . . . (There, it's beginning again, and I can't find appropriate words) two . . . arms, two . . . planes, no, I've got the word, for the object in question looks like a gigantic heron perched on one leg, with two wings —that's just it—two wings in gleaming metal with a total span of about six yards. As I can see, there are ten mechanisms conforming to this description ranged in battle array one beside the other. What ever can they be for?

When I'm satiated with this spectacle, I see that the company around us is fairly large.

First of all there's ex-lieutenant Lacour, recently promoted to the rank of Captain Rufus; the two former sergeants of our second escort, whose correct rank I do not know; their twenty black Tirailleurs, most of whom I recognize; and finally ten whites whom I've never before seen, who look rather like gallows-birds. If our society is numerous. I don't think it very choice.

In the middle of these gentry are my companions. They are all here, Miss Blazon is stretched on the ground. She is deathly white. Dr. Châtonnay and Malik, who is weeping copiously, are lavishing care upon her. Near her I can see St. Bérain, sitting on the ground and painfully regaining his breath. He's in a pitiable state. His bare skull is a brick-red, and his great eyes seem to be staring out of their orbits. Poor St. Bérain!

MM. Barsac and Poncin seem in better condition. They are standing, and exercising their joints. Why shouldn't I do likewise then?

But I can't see Tongané anywhere. Where can he be? Was he killed in the attack upon us? That's only too likely, and perhaps that's why Malik is sobbing so loudly. I, too, feel distressed, and I give a pitiful thought to the brave and faithful Tongané.

I get up and go towards Miss Blazon, without anyone saying anything to me. My legs are stiff, and I cannot move quickly. Captain Rufus precedes me.

"How's Mademoiselle Mornas?" he asks Dr. Châtonnay. Of course—Ex-lieutenant Lacour knows our fair comrade only under her borrowed name.

"Better," the doctor tells him. "Look she's opening her eyes."

"Can we get away?" asks the so-called captain.

"Not for an hour," Dr. Châtonnay declares firmly, "and what's more, unless you want to kill the lot of us, I advise you to adopt less barbarous methods than those you've been using so far."

Captain Rufus goes off without a reply. I walk up after him, and confirm that Miss Blazon is indeed returning to herself. Soon, helped by Dr. Châtonnay, who was kneeling beside her, she gets up. Then M. Barsac and M. Poncin come to join us. We are complete.

"Forgive me, my friends!" Miss Blazon says suddenly, great tears flowing from her eyes. "It was I who dragged you into this frightful predicament. But for me, you would still be safe. . . ."

We protest, as might well be supposed, but Miss Blazon goes on accusing herself and begging our pardon. Not being much given to self-pity, I think that these words are useless, and that it would be better to turn the conversation.

As Miss Blazon was known simply under the name of Mornas, I suggest it would be better to let her keep that pseudonym. Is it impossible, indeed, that there might be some of her brother's one-time followers among these rascals around us? If so, what's the use of incurring further danger, whatever it may be? This is approved unanimously. It is agreed that Miss Blazon will become Mlle Mornas, as before.

It's time we arrived at that conclusion, for our talk is suddenly interrupted. At a curt order from Captain Rufus, we are brutally seized. Three men devote themselves to my humble person. Once more I am trussed up and that disgusting sack again shuts me off from the outer world. Before I'm quite blindfolded, I realize that my companions, including Miss

B

Blazon—I beg her pardon, Mlle Mornas—are undergoing the same treatment. Then, as before, I'm carried off. . . . Am I going to resume that little horse-ride after the style of Mazeppa?

No. I am dumped face-downwards on some hard flat surface which doesn't at all resemble a horse's hide. Several minutes pass and I hear something like wings beating violently, while the surface which supports me begins to sway gently in all directions. This lasts a moment, then suddenly it's deafening— that famous roaring, but five times, ten times, a hundred times as loud, and then comes the wind striking me with an amazing force which increases from second to second. At the same time I have the feeling . . . how can I put it? . . . the feeling of being in a lift—or more precisely in a scenic railway, when the car rushes up and down artificial hills, when breathing is cut short, and the heart is seized with indescribable pain. . . . Yes, that's it, it's something of that sort I can feel.

This feeling lasts for perhaps five minutes, then, bit by bit, my body regains its usual equilibrium. At last, I declare, my head buried in that cursed sack, deprived of air and light, lulled by that roaring, which has now become regular, I think I must have fallen asleep.

A sudden surprise arouses me. One of my hands has moved. Yes, my bonds, insecurely fastened, have worked loose, and an unconscious effort has separated my hands.

At first I take care to keep still, for I'm not alone, as I learn from two voices howling through the surrounding din. Two people are talking. One speaks English, but in a voice so harsh it might have come from a gullet seared by alcohol. The other answers in the same language, but with a fantastic grammar, and mingled with words which I cannot understand. I guess they must come from the Bambara, for I often heard similar sounds during my four months in this lovely country. One of the two conversationalists is a true Englishman, the other is a negro. I can understand things less and less. Not that that matters, however. Whatever the colour of my guardians, the smallest movement of the sack must not let them suspect I've partly regained my freedom.

Slowly, carefully, I tug at my bonds, which gradually slide off my fists. Slowly, prudently, I succeed in moving my newly-freed hands along my body.

That's what I've done. Now I've got to see.

I've got something that will help me. In my pocket is a knife . . . no, not a knife, a pen-knife. It's so small that it eluded my captors, but though I couldn't use it as a weapon, it's large enough to open a tiny window in this stifling sack. Now I've got to get hold of it without attracting attention.

After a quarter of an hour of patient effort, I succeed.

Thus armed, I bring my right hand up to the level of my face, and pierce the sack.

Heavens! . . . What can I see! . . . . I could only just keep back a cry of surprise. My eyes, facing towards the ground, see it at an enormous distance below, more than five hundred yards I should think. The truth flashes upon me. I am in a flying machine, which is carrying me through the air with the speed of an express train, or perhaps even faster.

Hardly are they open when my eyes close. A shudder runs through me from head to heels. Under the impact of that surprise, I don't mind admitting I'm scared.

When my heart regains its regular beat, I can observe more calmly. The ground is rushing dizzily below my eyes. What speed are we making? A hundred, two hundred, miles an hour? More? Whatever the answer, the soil is that of the desert, sand mixed with pebbles, with fairly numerous clumps of dwarf palm-trees. A depressing country.

And yet I should have thought it would be worse. The dwarf palms are a bright green, and grass is growing abundantly between the pebbles. Contrary to general belief, does it rain sometimes in the desert?

Now and again I can make out, when they're below me, other contrivances like the one I'm in. My ears tell me that others are still higher. It is a flight of mechanical birds travelling through space. Serious though my position is, I get enthusiastic. It's a splendid sight, after all, and whoever our enemies may be, they are no ordinary people, those who have realized the ancient legend of Icarus in so masterly a fashion.

My field of view is not very great; so far as I can make out, thanks to slight movements which my guardians do not notice. I am looking between the plates of a metallic platform which restricts my view on every side. Because of our height, however, the view is fairly wide.

But here the countrys' changing. After about an hour's flight, I can suddenly see palm trees, meadows, gardens. It's an oasis, but a fairly small one, only about a yard across. No sooner do they appear than they vanish. But scarcely have we left one behind when another rises over the horizon before us, then after that there's a third, above which we're passing like a tornado.

Each of these oases only contains one house. A man comes out, attracted by the noise of our aerial apparatus. I don't see anybody else. Have these islets got only the one inhabitant?

Then a new problem confronts me, more insoluble still. Beyond the first oasis, our flying-machine follows a line of posts spaced out so regularly that I imagine them joined by a wire. I must be dreaming. The telegraph—unless it's the telephone—in the open desert?

After we pass the third oasis another, much more important, rises before us. I can see trees, not only palm-trees but several others, looking like karites, baobabs, acacias. I can also see cultivated fields, splendidly cultivated indeed, where a number of negroes are working. Then walls rise above the horizon towards which we are rushing. It's an unknown city we are approaching, for here's our fairy-bird starting to descend. Now here we are above it. It is only a moderately sized town but how queer! I can clearly make out semi-circular concentric streets, laid out on a rigorous plan. The central part is almost deserted, and at this time of day contains only a few negroes who hide in their huts when they hear the roaring of our machines. In the outer part, on the other hand, inhabitants are not lacking. They are whites who are looking upwards, and who—God forgive me—seem to be shaking their fists at us. I vainly ask myself what we've done to them.

But the machine carrying me descends more quickly. We cross a narrow river, then all at once I feel that we're falling like a stone. We're really describing a spiral which makes me feel sick. My heart is rising into my mouth. Where am I going? . . .

No, the roaring of the screw has stopped and our machine has touched down. For a few yards it glides over the surface with decreasing speed and then it stops.

A hand grasps the sack around my head and pulls it off. I have only just time to replace the bonds on my hands.

The sack removed, my limbs are freed. But whoever lets me loose has seen the trick.

"Who is the damned dog's son that has made this knot?" asks a drink-laden voice.

As you might think, I take care not to reply.

After my hands, my feet are unbound. I move them with a certain pleasure.

"Get up!" comes an authoritative order from someone I cannot see.

I don't ask to do anything else, but to obey is not easy. After the circulation of the blood has been checked so long, my limbs refuse to act. After a few fruitless attempts, I manage to succeed and I give a first glance at my surroundings.

Not very gay, the landscape. Before me is a high wall devoid of the smallest opening, and in the opposite direction the view is exactly identical. The same thing to my left. The scenery is not much diversified, to put it mildly! None the less, above the third wall I can see some sort of tower and a tall chimney. Can it be a factory? It is possible, in fact I think anything possible, except to imagine the use of that interminable pylon which rises and rises perhaps a hundred yards above the tower.

To my right the view is different but no more alluring. I

count two huge buildings, and in front of them is a great construction, a kind of fortress with outworks and crenellations.

My comrades in captivity are all here, unfortunately except for Tongané and except also for Malik, though she was present at this morning's halt. What's become of them?

Not having had, like myself, the advantage of enjoying a window opening on the countryside, my friends must be inconvenienced by the light. They can't see very much, for they keep blinking their eyes and rubbing them hard.

They are still rubbing them when a hand falls on the shoulder of each of us. We're dragged off, we're shoved, we are bewildered, discouraged. . . .

What do they want with us, and where the devil are we?

Alas! A minute later and we're in prison.

CHAPTER III

A DESPOT

(From the note-book of Amédée Florence)

26th March. Here I am then in prison. After having played
Mazeppa, I'm playing Silvio Pellico.[1]

As I've just stated, it was the day before yesterday, a little
before noon, when we were imprisoned. I was gripped by three
mulattos who, not without a certain brutality, forced me up
some stairs and then along a dark corridor leading out into a
long gallery with some cells opening from it. This gallery is
easy to guard, and sentinels are placed at both ends. I doubt
whether we shall be able to escape that way.

I'm thrust into a room lighted by a window reinforced with
an iron grille twelve feet above my head, and the door is
closed upon me and triply locked. I remain alone with my
thoughts, which are not exactly rose-coloured.

The cell is large and well ventilated. It contains a table with
writing materials, a chair, a bed which looks clean, and some
toilet utensils. An electric light bulb is fixed to the ceiling.
The "damp straw" of this dungeon is certainly comfortable,
and I should think this study quite ample—if I were free.

I sit down and light a cigarette. I wait—for what? For
something to happen. Meanwhile I reflect on the charms of
travel.

Two hours later I am aroused from my meditations by the
sound of my door opening. The bolts jar, the lock creaks, the
door gapes open, and I see. . . . I could give you a thousand
guesses.

I can see Tchoumouki, yes Tchoumouki, who vanished on
the day when, for the third time, I heard the mysterious roaring whose cause I now understand. He doesn't want for im-

---

[1] An Italian playwright and poet, a friend of Lord Byron; he wrote
an account of the ten years' imprisonment which he suffered through
being involved in a secret society, the Carbonari—I.O.E.

pudence. To dare to come in my presence after the way he treated my articles!

He is expecting rather a cool welcome himself. Before entering my cell, he glances in to see how the land lies. Much good may it do him.

"Oh, there you are, you double-dyed villain!" I exclaim as I dash towards him, with the idea of giving him the punishment he deserves.

But I come up against the door, which the traitor has hurriedly slammed. All the better, after all. When I promise myself the pleasure of pulling his ears, what good will that do me, except to complicate my position, which isn't too cheerful as it is?

Does he guess these more conciliatory thoughts? It seems like it, for the door opens a second time, so as to let the rascal shove his crinkly hair in. Oh, he can come in now. I've regained my chair . . . and my calm.

I repeat, but in a tone which doesn't convey a threat, "Oh, there you are, you double-dyed villain! What are you doing here?"

"Me have servant here," replies Tchoumouki, looking down shamefacedly as he opens the door wider.

In the corridor are two other negroes carrying some food; Tchoumouki sets it out on my table. The sight makes my mouth water, and I realize that I'm dying of hunger. That's not surprising. I'm still fasting, and it's now two in the afternoon.

Casting all care aside, I do justice to the meal, which Tchoumouki serves respectfully; I question him, and he makes no bones about replying. According to him I'm the guest—quite involuntary!—of a mighty king, Harry Killer—rather a nasty name, between ourselves—and he's had me brought to this extraordinary town, where "there are many big houses" and "many *toubab* things" which means it's full of European contrivances. I don't find this hard to believe, after my experiences in those prodigious flying-machines, which still amaze me.

I go on with my enquiry. It must be the king in question
who put him, Tchoumouki, in the path of Mlle Mornas, who
engaged him as guide, much as one chooses, in spite of himself, a conjurer's forced card. Tchoumouki says no, that he
was engaged without any mental reservations. He even main-
tains that he never broke his engagement and that he regards
himself as in the service of Mademoiselle Mornas and St.
Bérain so long as they stay in Africa. Is he mocking me? I look
at him. No, he speaks seriously, which has something rather
comical about it.

He says he was seduced by Moriliré, who himself was certainly in the pay of the monarch who's keeping us prisoner.
Not content with lavishing gold upon him, it seems that Moriliré had described in the most poetic terms the power and
generosity of this Harry Killer, whom Tchoumouki had never
seen, and had promised him a free and easy life. Such were
the reasons which made Tchoumouki turn his coat.

When I ask him if he knows what's become of his old
friend Tongané, his ugly face takes on a fierce look, he passes
his hand across his throat, and goes "Kwik!"

Then I've guessed right. Poor Tongané is stone dead.

Tchoumouki finishes his confidences. The roaring which I'd
heard on the day he vanished came from a flying-machine
which brought Lieutenant Lacour, or rather Captain Edward
Rufus. His men had come to meet us by the terrestrial route
under the command of the two N.C.O's, meanwhile amusing
themselves by plundering the villages they found in their way.
It was the skates of that flying machine which when it landed
had carved in the bush the grooves I'd seen next day while
out for my ride with Tongané.

This explains the unkempt appearance of the soldiers and
the impeccable elegance of the officer. It explains, too, the
terror of the negro wounded by the explosive bullet when he
recognized one of the men who'd attacked his village, in spite
of his indifference towards the so-called lieutenant, whom
he'd never before seen. As for him, Tchoumouki, he'd been

brought by the same machine when it returned to its port of departure, here, that is. . . .

He pronounces a name which he mangles terribly. By dint of much attention, I at last realize that he's trying to say "Blackland," a composite English word. This is quite plausible. So here we are at Blackland, a marvellous town according to Tchoumouki, although unknown to the best-informed geographers.

While the negro gives me this news, I ponder. As he has betrayed us for gain, why shouldn't he betray his new masters for the same reason? I approach him accordingly, and I mention a sum which would enable him to pass his whole life in delicious idleness. The rascal seems to find the proposal quite natural, but he shakes his head, like a man who doesn't see any chance of getting the prize.

"There no way of going," he tells me. "Here there many soldiers, many 'toubab things,' many big walls."

He adds that the town is surrounded by the desert, which we couldn't possibly cross. That's true, as I'd seen for myself when I traversed it by air. So are we condemned to remain here for the rest of our days?

The meal over, Tchoumouki goes, and I finish my day alone.

In the evening he serves my dinner—the cooking is quite good, in fact—then, just as my watch shows a few minutes past nine, the electric bulb suddenly goes out. I feel my way to bed.

After an excellent night, as I said, I get up on the 25th March and revise the notes describing the vicissitudes of our kidnapping and our aerial voyage. The day is spent peacefully. I do not see anybody except Tchoumouki, who serves my meals regularly. In the evening, taught by experience, I go to bed earlier. I can congratulate myself. At the same hour as before, the light goes out. It's evidently a rule of the house.

Another good night, and here I am once more, this morning, the 26th of March, fresh and cheerful, but alas! still a prisoner. The position is absurd, for what do they want with us? When shall I see someone I can ask?

In the evening. My wishes have been fulfilled. We have seen His Majesty Harry Killer, and our situation has undergone important alterations since that interview, which has left me still moved, still trembling.

It might be three in the afternoon when the door opened. This time it was not Tchoumouki who hid behind it but another of our old friends, Morilire. He is accompanied by a score of negroes whom he seems to command.

In the midst of that troop I can see my companions, including Miss Blazon-Mornas, but not including St. Bérain, who still can't be moved, so his young aunt says. I go and join them, thinking my last hour has come, and we're being taken off to the execution shed.

Nothing of the sort. We follow a series of corridors, and at last arrive at a fairly large room. We enter, while our escort waits on the threshold.

The room is furnished only with an arm-chair in palm fibre and a table bearing a glass and a bottle half filled, which emits the smell of alcohol. The arm-chair is behind the table and in it sits a man. Our eyes converge on that man. He's worth it.

His Majesty Harry Killer must be about forty-five years old, though there are some signs that he's older. As far as we can tell, he is tall, and his sturdy build, his enormous hands, his stout muscular limbs, show an uncommon, not to say an Herculean, strength.

But it is his head which especially attracts attention. His face is hairless, and indicates a complex character, at once powerful and villainous. He is crowned by dishevelled greying hair, a veritable mane which from time immemorial seems to have had a quarrel with the comb. His forehead, whence the hair has retreated, is broad and suggests intelligence, but his protruding jaw and heavy square chin indicate coarse and violent passions. His cheeks, deeply bronzed, and with prom-

inent bones, cave inwards, then hang down in two heavy lobes;
they bear scattered pimples so red they almost resemble blood.
His mouth is thick-lipped and his lower lip, slightly hanging
down, discloses strong teeth, healthy but yellow and badly
cleaned. His eyes, deeply sunk in their orbits and surmounted
by bristling eyebrows, have an extraordinary and sometimes,
indeed, almost an unbearable brilliance.

This personage is certainly not at all commonplace. Every
appetite, every vice, every audacity, are surely his. Hideous,
yes, but formidable.

His Majesty is clad in a sort of hunting outfit of grey cloth,
breeches, leggings and tunic, all filthy and covered with stains.
On the table he has placed a large woollen hat; near this is
his right hand, which is in a continual tremble.

Out of the corner of his eye, Dr. Châtonnay indicates that
shaking hand. I understand what he would like to say: it's
an alcoholic, almost a drunkard, whom we have before us.

For some time that individual considers us in silence. His
eyes go from one to the other, and pass us successively in
review. We await his good pleasure patiently.

"They told me there are six of you," he says at last, in
French but with a strong English accent, speaking in a stern
but raucous voice. "I can only see five. Why?"

"One of us is ill," replies Dr. Châtonnay, "ill from the
sufferings your men inflicted on him."

There is a fresh interval of silence, then our interlocutor gets
up suddenly and asks *ex abrupto:* "What did you come to my
country for?"

The question is so unexpected that in spite of the gravity of
the situation we all want to laugh. Well! If we are in his
country, it is in spite of ourselves.

He goes on, with a menacing look. "To spy, no doubt."

"Excuse me, Sir" . . . says M. Barsac.

But the other interrupts him. Seized by a sudden anger, he
crashes his fist on the table and roars in a voice of thunder:
"They call me Master."

M. Barsac then becomes superb. An orator always and even now, he draws himself up, places his left hand on his heart, and sweeps the air with a wide movement of his right arm : "Since seventeen hundred and eighty-nine," he declares emphatically, "the French have never had a master."

Anywhere else it would evoke laughter, I admit, this somewhat melodramatic declaration of M. Barsac, but in the present circumstances, in the teeth of this sort of wild beast, I assure you it is not without nobility. It shows that we shall never consent to humble ourselves before this drunken adventurer. We all applaud the speaker, down to M. Poncin; carried away with his enthusiasm, he cries : "Take away a man's independence ,and you take his freedom !"

Gallant M. Poncin ! Certainly he means well.

On hearing this indisputable statement, Harry Killer shrugs his shoulders. Then he again starts staring at us in turn, as though he had never seen us before. His eyes pass from one to another with amazing speed. He stops at last with M. Barsac, at whom he darts a most terrible look. M. Barsac does not flinch. My congratulations. That son of the Midi, he's not only voluble, he has courage and dignity too. The chief of our Mission is rising in my esteem by leaps and bounds.

Harry Killer succeeds in controlling himself, which cannot happen every day, then with a calmness as unexpected as his anger was sudden, he says : "Do you speak English ?"

"Yes," M. Barsac replies.

"And your companions."

"Just as well."

"Good," Harry Killer agrees; then in the same half-drunken voice he repeats his previous question in English : "What have you come here for ?"

The answer is obvious.

"It's for us to ask you that question," M. Barsac replies, "and to demand what right you've got to keep us here by force."

"Because I've got you," snaps Harry Killer his fury suddenly

going beyond all bounds. "While I'm alive, nobody comes
near my empire!"

His empire? . . . I don't follow this.

Harry Killer jumps up. Especially addressing M. Barsac,
who still looks very firm, he continues in furious tones and
hammering the table with his gigantic fist : "Yes, yes, I know
well enough that your countrymen have reached Timbuctoo
and keep working their way up the Niger, but they'd better
stop. If they don't. . . . And now they've got the impudence to
send spies to the river by land! . . . I'll smash them, your spies,
just as I smash this glass!"

And, adding gesture to speech, Harry Killer does in fact
smash his glass, which shatters to pieces on the floor.

"Another glass!" he howls, turning towards the door.

Carried away by incredible fury, literally maddened with
rage, for a little foam oozes from the corners of his lips, he is
not good to look at now. His projecting lower jaw makes him
resemble a wild beast with his purple face and his bloodshot
eyes.

One of the Black Guard has hastened to obey him. Without troubling about him, the man, as though he were possessed,
leaning on the table which his hands are beating violently,
turns towards the unmoved M. Barsac, fixes him with his eyes
and shouts :

"And didn't I give you enough warning? . . . That yarn
about the *doung-kono,* which I'd thought up for your benefit,
that was the first hint. It was I who placed in your path that
fortune-teller and it's your own fault his warning's been fulfilled. It was I who sent you your guide, my slave Moriliré, to
make a last effort to stop you at Sikasso. But it was all in vain.
In vain I took away your escort, in vain I starved you out—
nothing would suit you but to push on the Niger. . . . Well,
you've reached the Niger, you've even crossed the Niger, and
you've found out what you wanted to know. . . . And much
you've got for it! Now how are you going to tell this to your
paymasters?"

In the grip of this boundless fury, Harry Killer is parading up and down. To my mind there's no doubt about it—he's mad. Suddenly he stops, his mind seized by an unexpected idea : "But, as a matter of fact," he asks M. Barsac, with surprising calm, "weren't you really aiming for Saye?"

"Yes," M. Barsac replies.

"Then why did you go off in quite a different direction? What were you going to do at Koubo?"

Harry Killer accompanies this question with a piercing look, while we exchange embarrassed glances. The question is certainly troublesome, as we have agreed not to mention Miss Blazon's real name. Fortunately M. Barsac finds a plausible reply. "As our escort deserted us," he says, "we were making for Timbuctoo."

"Why not for Sikasso? That's not so far."

"We simply thought it best to make for Timbuctoo."

"H'm," grunts Harry Killer doubtfully, then after a brief silence he continues : "Then you didn't mean to go eastwards to the Niger?"

"No," M. Barsac assures him.

"If I could have guessed that," Harry Killer informs us, "you wouldn't be here now."

What a joke! As if he'd taken the trouble to ask us!

Profiting by the silence following this preposterous remark, I take up the conversation. I—I who write this—am a very logical person. Anything which isn't reasonable shocks me, like an untidy cupboard. And in this record there's one point which intrigues me. So I put in my spoke :

"Excuse me, dear Sir," I say, with exquisite courtesy, "I'd like to know why you took the trouble to fetch us here, instead of simply wiping us out. Your Captain Edward Rufus and his men had the whip hand of us for we'd no reason to mistrust them. Surely it would have been the best way of getting rid of us."

Harry Killer knitted his brows and looked at me disdainfully. Who was this pigmy who dared address him? All the same, he deigns to reply : "So as to avoid an investigation by the French authorities. They would certainly have been perturbed if one of their Missions had been wiped out."

I'm partly satisfied. Not quite, however. I raise an objection : "I should think it would have the same effect if we vanished."

"Of course," admits Harry Killer, who for once is showing sound common sense. "So I'd have preferred to see you abandon your journey. It's only your obstinacy which made me bring you here."

He's offered me a chance, which I seize at once. "Then we can arrange everything," I suggest. "You understand now that we don't at all want to go to the Niger, so you've only got to put us back where you found us, and then there won't be any question. . . ."

"So that you can go and spread abroad what you've found out? So that you can reveal the existence of this town that nobody has ever heard of?" Harry Killer breaks in violently. "No, it's too late. Nobody who enters Blackland will ever leave it."

But he can wear his throat out as much as he likes. I'm getting used to his storming. I pay no attention to that, and I insist : "But an enquiry will be held?"

"Very likely," Harry Killer replies, his barometer needle now having returned to set fair. "But my position will be better. If I am found out, and if I have to fight, at any rate I shall have something better than your dead bodies."

"What's that?"

"Hostages."

He's in a strong position, this potentate. He's quite right. But I was right, too, to interview him, because his replies show he's no intention of putting us to death on the spot. That's always good to know.

Harry Killer has resumed his seat in his arm-chair behind the table. He's a disconcerting fellow. Here he is now, perfectly calm and fully in control of himself.

"Let's make ourselves clear," he says, in icy tones which are new to us. "You are in Blackland, and you're not going out again, not one of you. As to the sort of life you lead, that will be what you make it. I'm not responsible to anyone. I can keep you in prison or wipe you out, if I want to, just as I can let you have the same freedom I enjoy myself, within the limits of my empire."

That word again. He disfigures it.

"That will depend on you," he continues, addressing himself first and foremost to M. Barsac, whom he certainly regards as our leader. "You can either be my hostages or. . . ."

He strikes an attitude. M. Barsac looks at him with an astonishment which I share. What else can we be, then?

"Or my collaborators," Harry Killer ends coldly.

To say that this proposal surprises us would be an understatement. We are absolutely thunder-struck.

However, he goes on just as coldly : "You mustn't think I'm under any illusion about the progress of the French Forces. If they don't yet know about my existence, they'll learn of it very forcibly some day. Then I'll have either to fight or to bargain. Don't think I'm afraid to fight. I'm quite able to defend myself. But war isn't the only possible solution. To colonize the Niger Bend will keep France busy for a long while. What good would it do them to risk a defeat simply to push on further eastwards in spite of me across an ocean of sand which I'm converting into fertile fields? Properly conducted, our negotiations might end in an alliance."

He takes a lot for granted, this fellow! He's oozing vanity from every pore. Can anyone see the French Republic entering into an alliance with this loathsome tyranny?

"With you?" the amazed exclamation of M. Barsac expresses the thought of us all.

It takes no more than this to unchain the tempest. Indeed, the calm has already lasted too long. It was beginning to get monotonous.

"Perhaps you don't think I'm worth it?" roars Harry Killer, his eyes blazing, as he hammers anew on his unoffending table. "Or perhaps you're hoping to escape? That's because you don't realize my power."

He gets up, and adds in threatening tones : "You'll know better soon !"

The guards enter at his call. They grab hold of us, they drag us off. We go up endless stairways, then they make us promenade along a great terrace, followed by more staircases. We emerge at last on the platform of a tower, where Harry Killer is not slow to join us.

The man fluctuates lke a wave. No half-measures with him. He passes without transition from a mad fury to an icy calm, and back again. For the time being there's not a vestige of his last outbreak.

"You're forty yards high here," he says, the tone of a guide explaining a view. "So the horizon is about fifteen miles away. You can understand that, so far as your eyes can see, the desert which surrounds us has been replaced by a fertile countryside. The empire I rule covers more than six hundred square miles at least. Really it is about twelve hundred. That's the work we've carried out over ten years."

Harry Killer interrupts himself for a moment. When he has preened himself enough—certainly not without reason this time—he goes on : "If anyone tried to enter these twelve hundred square miles. I should get immediate warning from a triple line of outposts set up in the desert, and connected to the Palace by telephone. . . ."

So that's the explanation of the oases and the telegraph poles which I saw the other day. But let's listen to Harry Killer, who is showing us a sort of glass lantern, something like that of a lighthouse but far larger, raised in the midst of the platform.

He continues in the same tone. "If that isn't enough, nobody could enter without my permission; he could not cross a protective zone half a mile wide, placed five furlongs outside the walls of Blackland, because it is swept all night by rays from powerful projectors. Thanks to its optical structure, this

instrument, which I call the cycloscope, looks directly down-
wards on that circle of territory so that the look-out at its
centre can keep every detail under his eyes—and enormously
enlarged, too. Come into the cycloscope—I give you permission—and judge for yourselves."

Our curiosity much aroused, we profit by this permission,
and enter the lantern through a door consisting of an enormous lens swinging on hinges under our eyes. No sooner do we
enter than the outside world changes. To whatever side we
turn, we can see at first nothing but an upright wall, divided
into a number of separate squares by a grille of black lines.

This wall, whose base is separated from us by a gulf of
shadows, and whose top seems to tower above us to a prodigious height, apparently consists of a sort of milky light. Then
we begin to realize that its colour, far from being uniform, is
compounded from countless patches of different shades with
rather vague outlines. A little attention shows us that some of
these patches are trees, others are fields or roads, and others
again people working on the land, all enlarged so much we
can recognize them easily.

"You see those negroes," asks Harry Killer, pointing to two
widely separated stains. "Suppose they took it into their heads
to escape. They wouldn't get far !"

While speaking, he has picked up the telephone transmitter.
"Hundred and eleven circle. Radius fifteen hundred and
twenty-eight."

Then, picking up another transmitter, he adds : "Fourteen
circle. Radius fifteen hundred and two."

Then, turning towards us, "Look carefully at this," he tells
us.

After a few minutes wait, during which nothing special
happens, one of the patches is obscured by a cloud of smoke.
When this has cleared, the patch has vanished.

"What's happened to the man working there?" asks Mlle
Mornas in a voice trembling with emotion.

"He's dead," Harry Killer replies coldly.

"Dead! . . ." We exclaim. "You've killed that poor fellow for no reason at all?"

"Don't worry, he's only a negro," Harry Killer explains with perfect simplicity. "Mere trash. When there aren't any of them left we can get more. That one was wiped out by an aerial torpedo. It's a sort of rocket which carries up to fifteen miles, and you've seen its accuracy and speed."

While we are listening to his explanation, so far at least as the distress aroused by this abominable cruelty allows us, something has entered into our field of view. It sped rapidly along the milky wall, and the second patch has also vanished.

"What about that man?" asks Mlle Mornas, hardly able to speak, "Is he dead, too?"

"No," replies Harry Killer, "that one's still alive. You're going to see him in a moment."

He goes out, followed by our guard, who thrust us outside. Now we are once again on the platform of the tower. We look around, and some distance away we see coming towards us, with the speed of a shooting-star, an apparatus like that which brought us here. Suspended beneath its lower surface we can see something swinging.

"Here's the heliplane," Harry Killer thus tells us the name of the flying-machine. "In less than a minute you'll understand whether anyone can get in or out of this place against my wishes."

The heliplane indeed approaches us quickly. It looms larger in our sight. We suddenly tremble : the object swinging below it—it is a negro, whom a sort of giant pincers has seized in the middle of his body.

The heliplane comes nearer still. It passes above the tower. . . . Horrible! The pincers have opened, and the wretched negro has just smashed at our feet. From his shattered head the brains have spurted in every direction, and we are spattered with blood.

A cry of indignation escapes us. But Mlle Mornas is not satisfied with a cry, she acts. Her eyes flashing, pale, her lips bloodless, she thrusts aside the startled warders and hurls herself upon Harry Killer.

"You coward! . . . You wretched murderer! . . ." she cries to his face, while her small hands knot themselves around the villian's neck.

He frees himself effortlessly, and we tremble for the foolhardy girl. Alas! We can do nothing to aid her. The guards have seized us and hold us helpless.

Fortunately the dictator does not seem to have, for the time at any rate, any intention of punishing our brave companion, whom two men have dragged back. If his mouth is set in a cruel grimace, something like a look of pleasure comes into his eyes; he fixes them on the young girl who is still trembling.

"Well, well," he says, in a fairly good-humoured tone, "she's got spirit, the filly."

Then thrusting his foot against the remains of the wretched negro he adds, "you shouldn't worry about trifles, little girl."

He goes down, we are hustled after him, and we are taken back into that room, so well furnished with a table and one solitary chair, which I shall accordingly speak of in future as the Throne Room. Harry Killer takes his place on the said throne and looks at us.

When I say that he's looking at us. . . . To tell the truth, he's only paying attention to Mlle Mornas. He fixes her with his menacing eyes, into which there gradually comes an evil light.

"You'll realize my power now," he says at last, "and I've shown you that my offers are not to be sneezed at. I renew them for the last time. I'm told that among you are a politician, a doctor, a journalist, and two half-wits. . . ."

For M. Poncin, agreed! But for poor St. Bérain, what an injustice!

"If need be, the politician can negotiate with France, I shall build a hospital for the doctor, the journalist can work on the *Blackland Thunderbolt*, and I'll find a way of using the two others. There remains the child. I like her . . . I'll marry her."

Our consternation may well be imagined to hear so unexpected a conclusion. But, with a madman! . . .

"None of that will happen," M. Barsac replies firmly. "The abominable crimes of which you've made us the witnesses haven't shaken us. We shall submit to force because we have to, but never shall we consent to be anything more than your prisoners or your victims. As for Mlle Mornas. . . ."

"Oh, it's Mornas that my future wife is called, is it?" Harry Killer interrupts him.

"Whether I call myself Mornas or not," cries our comrade, absolutely wild with anger, "understand that I regard you as a wild beast, as contemptible as you are disgusting, and I regard your proposal as an insult—the vilest, the most shameful, the most. . . ."

The voice chokes in her throat. As for Harry Killer, he merely laughs. The wind's certainly blowing towards mercy.

"That's fine . . . that's fine . . ." he says. "No hurry. You can all have a month to consider it."

But the barometer has fallen, and the good weather is over. He gets up and turns towards his guards. "Take them away!" he cries in a voice of thunder.

For a moment M. Barsac resists the guards who are hustling him. He turns to Harry Killer. "And, in a month's time, what are you going to do with us?" he asks.

But the wind has changed already. The dictator is no longer thinking about us, and his trembling hand lifts to his mouth a glass of alcohol which he's going to drink. At M. Barsac's question, he takes the glass from his lips, then, without any signs of anger, he says in indecisive tones and raising his eyes towards the ceiling: "I don't quite know—perhaps I shall have you hanged."

CHAPTER IV

FROM 26th MARCH TO 8th APRIL

As AMÉDÉE FLORENCE explained in his notes, after their
interview with Harry Killer the six prisoners emerged in consternation. The death of those two wretched negroes, and
especially the frightful end of the second, had distressed them
greatly. How could such beings exist, so fierce that they inflicted so much suffering for no reason, for a mere whim,
simply to demonstrate their detestable power?

None the less an agreeable surprise awaited them. Harry
Killer, who had just allowed them a month to consider their
position, no doubt sought to win them over by considerate
treatment. Whatever the reason, the doors of their cells were
no longer locked as before, and they were now free to move
at will about the gallery. This became their common-room,
where they could meet as often as they liked.

From one end of the gallery rose a staircase which opened,
at the floor immediately above, on to the top of the bastion
which contained their cells. They were similarly allowed to
enjoy the freedom of this platform. If, during the hours of
tropical sunshine, they did not wish to take advantage of this,
they very much appreciated the pleasure of spending their
evenings in the open air; there they could stay as long as they
wished, without anyone's commenting on it.

In such conditions life was on the whole not too irksome,
and they were as happy as the loss of their freedom and as
their anxiety about the future would allow. The group of
cells, the gallery, and the terrace formed a real self-contained
apartment, except for the closed door at the far end of the
gallery. Behind that door were stationed their jailors. The
voices of these, the clashing of their arms, reminded the
prisoners that this boundary was not to be crossed.

Domestic service was seen to by Tchoumouki, who showed
the greatest zeal. Nevertheless, they saw him only when he

55

was waiting on them. Outside the hours devoted to the cleaning of their cells and to their meals he was never there, and they did not have to endure the presence of that rascal to whom, in part at any rate, they owed their unfortunate circumstances.

During the day they visited one another, or prowled up and down along the gallery; then, at sunset, they ascended to the platform, where Tchoumouki would sometimes serve dinner.

The square-shaped bastion in which they were incarcerated formed the western angle of the Palace, and on two sides it dominated the broad terrace. It was separated from this by a series of interior yards, which they had crossed to reach the central tower where they had seen the cycloscope. Of its two other façades, one rose above the Esplanade between the Palace and the Factory; this esplanade was bounded towards the Red River by an immense wall, to which the other façade formed an extension, towering above the river to a height of about ninety feet.

Hence they had to regard any idea of escape as impossible. Not to mention the difficulty of evading the surveillance whose efficacy Harry Killer had so cruelly demonstrated, they could not so much as dream of leaving the Palace. To get from the bastion to the terrace, which was continually traversed by the Counsellors and the Merry Fellows on duty and by the negroes of the domestic staff and the Black Guard, would have availed them nothing, even if such a feat were possible. Nor would much be gained by escaping from the Esplanade, bounded on all sides by insurmountable walls. The Red River offered the only hope of escape, but the prisoners possessed neither a boat nor any method of descending the ninety feet drop into it.

From the height of the platform they could follow with their eyes the course of the Red River. Up and down stream, this vanished between rows of trees, already of respectable height although they had not yet been planted ten years. Except for the public Garden, hidden by the Palace, the whole of Blackland was spread out before their eyes. They could see the three sections bounded by their lofty walls, the concentric semi-circular streets, the western and eastern quarters, with their sparse population of whites, and the centre where there swarmed, at dawn, an immense crowd before it went out to spread over the surrounding countryside.

Their view extended into part of the Factory, but what they could see gave them very little light on that second town, enclosed within the first, and seeming to have no communication with this.

What was the purpose of these workshops, surmounted by a chimney which emitted not even a vestige of smoke, and by a tower like that of the Palace, but lengthened to a height of over a hundred yards, by that inexplicable pylon which Amédée Florence had noticed the moment he arrived? What was the meaning of those immense buildings, towering in the expanse beside the Red River, and many clothed in a thick layer of grass-covered earth? What needs did that other tract answer, the largest of all, which contained market and fruit gardens? Why that metallic revetment above the high wall which bounded it in? Why, at its base, that wide deep trench? Why, indeed, that wall—for its two sides gave neither on to the River nor on to the Esplanade with its outer wall, beyond which began the open country? Somebody had apparently meant to give that tiny city its own special defences, and to bar it from any communication with the outer world. The whole thing was inexplicable.

When questioned, Tchoumouki had not been able to supply the name of this inner city. "Work House," was all he said, mangling the words terribly as though he had a superstitious fear of them. Indeed, as one of Harry Killer's latest recruits, he did not understand very much, and he himself could not have given any reason for the terror he showed, which indeed was only the reflection of the general feeling in the town. Plainly some power must be hidden behind that unbroken wall which faced the Palace. What was its nature? Could they ever succeed in understanding it, and could they possibly use it for their own ends?

The freedom of Jane Blazon had been extended even more widely. By order of Harry Killer, Tchoumouki had told her that she could come and go unhindered, and without any fear for her safety, either in the Palace or on the Esplanade. She was merely forbidden to cross the Red River, and she could not have done this anyhow, as a post of the Merry Fellows was always on guard at the Castle Bridge.

Needless to say, she had not taken advantage of the privilege. Whatever happened, she would share the same fate as her companions in misfortune. She remained as much a prisoner as they. This greatly astonished Tchoumouki, who thought magnificent the plans made for his former employer.

"You not good stay prison," he told her. "When you marry Master, it be good. He give you *toubabs*."

But Jane Blazon only turned a deaf ear to this negroid advocacy, and Tchoumouki got nothing for his feats of eloquence.

When they were not together in the gallery or on the bastion, the prisoners occupied their leisure each according to his own taste.

Barsac was weak enough to pride himself beyond all bounds on the firmness of his attitude towards Harry Killer. The well-deserved compliments it brought him had inflated his vanity, and he was prepared, regardless of consequences, to seek for more. As with him every impulse took an oratorical form, he had never stopped working, since then, on the speech which he would hurl at the tyrant on the first opportunity, and he polished and repolished the vengeful tirade which he would improvise and throw in his face the moment he dared repeat his dishonourable offers.

Dr. Châtonnay and St. Bérain, now freed from his lumbago, were both somewhat at a loss, the one because he had no patients, the other because circumstances made it impossible for him to carry on his favourite sport; they usually spent their time with Jane Blazon and tried to console her. The memory of her father, left solitary in Glenor Castle, still distressed the girl, although she now felt herself in a position to lessen the old man's inconsolable despair. How could she take him the proof, still incomplete but certainly cogent, of George Blazon's innocence?

Amédée Florence spent much of his time in editing his notes. Not a day passed without his performing this professional duty. If he ever again had the chance of seeing Europe, at least the adventures of the Barsac Missions should be known in their most intimate details.

As for M. Poncin, he said nothing and did nothing, except from time to time to jot down in his voluminous note-book one of those cabalistic annotations which still so greatly intrigued Amédée Florence.

"Would I be indiscreet, Monsieur Poncin," he ventured one day to his silent companion, "to ask you what you are noting so carefully?"

The face of M. Poncin lit up. Indeed no, that wouldn't be indiscreet. On the other hand, he would be greatly flattered if any noticed his work and appreciated its interest.

"At the moment I'm working out problems," he said portentously.

"Bah!" said the reporter.

"Yes, Monsieur. I'm trying to solve this : 'A is twice as old as B was when A was as old as B is now. When B is as old as A is now, the total of their ages will be N years. How old are A and B? Representing the age of A by X. . . .'"

"But that's not a problem, it's a Chinese puzzle," cried Amédée Florence. "Does that sort of thing amuse you?"

"It's my passion. That special problem is particularly elegant. I've been working on it since I was a child, without ever getting tired of it."

"Since you were a child?" Florence repeated in amazement.

"Yes, Monsieur," M. Poncin affirmed, not without a certain

vanity. "To-day I've arrived at my 1197th solution, which makes A 4798 years old and B 3691 years."

"Not what you'd call young," remarked Amédée Florence without flinching. "But the other 1196 solutions. . . ."

"They're just as accurate. Every multiple of 9 satisfies the equation, so the number of solutions is infinite. If I lived ten thousand years I should never reach the end of them. So if you represent the age of A by x and that of B by y. . . ."

"No, no, Monsieur Poncin," interrupted Florence rather scared. "I'd rather suggest another problem, which at any rate will have the charm of novelty."

"With pleasure," replied M. Poncin; pencil in hand, he prepared to note down the details.

"Three people," Amédée Florence dictated, "one six feet four inches tall, the second five feet eight inches, and the third a foot tall, have gone twenty miles in twenty-four hours. How many miles a second will eight people go if two of them are lame, granted that their average age is forty-five?"

"It's a rule of three problem," said M. Poncin, wrinkling up his brows as he considered it.

"You can work it out at your leisure," Amédée Florence hastened to advise him. "Now, was that the sort of calculation you were noting down all the time we were travelling?"

"Not at all, Monsieur Florence," M. Poncin protested, looking very impressive. "Such problems are only my hobby, a mere pastime. I usually busy myself with questions much more important than that, I ask you to believe."

"May I?"

"I'm a statistician," M. Poncin admitted with feigned modesty.

"Then that's full of statistics?" asked Amédée Florence indicating the famous pocket-book.

"Yes, Monsieur," replied M. Poncin, absolutely drunk with enthusiasm. "These notes form a mine of inexhaustible information, Monsieur! I've discovered some astonishing facts!"

M. Poncin had opened his note-book, and was thumbing through its pages.

"Look at this, Monsieur," he exclaimed, pointing to an entry dated the 16th February. After mentioning the number of antelopes they had seen, he continued : "It thus results math-em-at-ic-al-ly that the 25,000 square miles at which I estimate the area of the Niger Bend would contain 556,055 antelopes and .842 of an antelope. There's information which is worth something from a zoological point of view, I fancy !"

"Indeed . . . indeed. . . ." babbled Amédée Florence, astounded.

"Amazing things, I tell you," M. Poncin continued volubly with some statistics which culminated in the statement, "And the tatto-marks of the negroes of this region, placed end to end, would make the 103,589ths of the circuit of the earth ! That. . . ."

"That's enough! that's enough! . . . Monsieur Poncin," Florence interrupted him, holding his ears. "It is certainly fine, but I declare it's too much for me. A last question—these hieroglyphics, which I took the liberty of copying one day, are they anything of the sort?"

"Precisely," M. Poncin declared, and he explained some of his cabalistics : "What's most interesting is the conclusion, the total population of the Niger Bend. As you see, on 5th December, P.t., that means the total population—1,479,114."

"Yes, I understand," said Florence, "but I also notice that, at 16th February, P.t. 470,652. Which of these numbers is right?"

"Both," declared M. Poncin. "The first was true for the 5th December, and the second for the 16th February."

"Then some frightful epidemic must have taken place in between?"

"I don't know and I don't want to know," was the sublime declaration of M. Poncin. "A statistician worthy of the name refuses to consider causes, Monsieur. He watches, he observes, he counts, it all lies in that. Then, from his observations, his investigations, his estimates, the results emerge spontaneously. What does it matter if they change? That is math-em-at-ic-al-ly inevitable, if their factors have altered. A detail like that does not keep addition from being addition, subtraction from being subtraction, multiplication. . . ."

"From being multiplication, etcetera."

"Etcetera," M. Poncin repeated mechanically. "Statistics may be an immutable science, Monsieur, but it is forever evolving."

His curiosity more fully satisfied than he had expected, after this admirable maxim, Amédée Florence hastened to close the discussion.

When the prisoners were together the subject of their conversation was more serious. As might be thought, they usually discussed their situation and the man it depended on. This was Harry Killer; time did not detract from the impression he had made upon them.

"Who can that fellow be?" asked M. Barsac.

"He's English," replied Jane Blazon. "His accent shows that."

"English, granted," Barsac answered, "but that doesn't tell us much. Anyhow, he's no ordinary man. To have created a town, to have transformed the desert as he has done, to have brought water to regions where it has been unknown for centuries, and all in ten years, this work presupposes a veritable genius making use of a vast scientific knowledge. It's not conceivable that this adventurer has such marvellous gifts."

"I find it more incomprehensible still," said Amédée Florence. "I think Harry Killer is mad."

"He's half-mad, at least," Dr. Châtonnay corrected him. "But he's a half-mad alcoholic, and that's terrible."

"These two qualities together," said Amédée Florence, "makes him the classical type of the despot, a creature of impulse, whom fate has endowed with power, and who uses it like a spoiled child. Unable to tolerate the slightest opposition, he passes without any transition from fury to calmness and back again, and he shows a profound contempt for human life, as others understand it."

"Such a character is not uncommon in Africa," Dr. Châtonnay explained. "To live continually in the company of men generally inferior to themselves, to be able to order them about uncontrolled, too often makes cruel satraps out of Europeans who haven't a firm enough character and lofty enough ideals to keep them from being seduced. Despotism is an endemic disease of the Colonies. Harry Killer has taken it a little further, that's all."

"So far as I'm concerned, he's mad, I tell you," Amédée Florence summed up the discussion, "and you can never trust a madman. I'm sure that he's forgotten us, and yet I can't deny that within five minutes he might order us to be executed on the spot."

For a week his pessimistic conjectures were not realized, and until the 3rd April life went on without anything fresh happening. That day, was however, marked by two events of a very different nature. About three in the afternoon the prisoners were agreeably surprised at the arrival of Malik. As soon as she saw Jane Blazon, Malik fell at her feet and kissed, with touching warmth, the hands of her good mistress, who was equally moved herself.

It transpired that, instead of being transported by heliplane like the other prisoners, the little negress had come, with fourteen men and the two sergeants of the former escort, by stages during which she had not escaped harsh treatment. Nobody asked her about the fate of Tongané, of whom, to judge by her distress, she had no news.

Two hours after her arrival came a second incident of a very different nature. It was about five when Tchoumouki ran into the gallery. Showing signs of great agitation, he told the prisoners that Harry Killer had sent him with orders to fetch Mlle Mornas, whom The Master regarded as his future wife.

The prisoners were unanimous in their downright refusal, and in spite of his insistence Tchoumouki had to retire. As soon as he had gone, they excitedly discussed Harry Killer's strange invitation. All were in agreement on this point, that their companion should not be separated from them on any pretext.

"Thank you, friends," Jane Blazon told them, "for the gallant protection you've thrown round me, but don't think I shan't be able to protect myself when I'm alone with that brute—after all he isn't invulnerable. Though they've searched you, they didn't think it worth while to take that precaution with a woman, and they've left me this weapon."

Jane showed them the dagger she had found in her brother's grave, and was now carrying hidden in her clothing.

"Be sure," she added, "if necessary, I shall know how to use it."

Scarcely had she put the weapon back in its hiding-place when Tchoumouki returned, almost mad with fear. On hearing Mlle Mornas' reply Harry Killer had got into a furious rage, and had sent him to fetch her immediately. If she persisted in her refusal, all six of the prisoners would be hanged at once.

Hesitation was no longer possible, and Jane Blazon, refusing to bring such a fate on those whom she had let into this adventure, insisted, in spite of her companions' entreaties, on complying. They vainly tried to hold her back by force. At Tchoumouki's shout, a dozen negroes burst into the gallery and kept them helpless until she had gone.

She did not return until eight that evening, after an absence of three long hours while her companions—especially the unhappy St. Bérain, who was weeping copiously—felt the greatest uneasiness on her account.

"Well?" they asked, as soon as they saw her.

"Well, that's well over," replied the girl, who was still trembling.

"What did he want with you?"

"Nothing—or rather, he wanted to see me, that's all. When I got there, he had already begun drinking, which seems to be his custom, and he was half drunk. He made me sit down, and began to pay compliments to me, after his usual style. He told me that he found me to his taste, and that he'd like to have a little housewife like me. He boasted of his power and his wealth, which he said are immense, and which I should enjoy like him when I was his wife.

"I listened to him quietly, and merely replied that he had given us a month to consider things, and that so far only a week had elapsed. Strange as you may think it, he was not at all offended; I really think I've got some influence over the madman. He agreed that he would allow us a month to make up our minds, but on condition that I devote all my afternoons to him. . . ."

"Then you've got to go back there, my poor child?" St. Bérain cried distressfully.

"It's absolutely necessary," Jane Blazon replied, "but I don't think I shall be risking much, to judge by our first afternoon. He was completely drunk before seven, and my task was simply to light his pipe and fill his glass until the brute began to snore, when I took the opportunity of coming back to you."

Thenceforth, indeed, she had to go every day, about three, to Harry Killer, with whom she stayed until about eight. According to her report every evening, the treaty was peaceably complied with. She spent every afternoon in the same manner. On her arrival she found the despot in conference with his Counsellors, and the orders he gave them certainly showed great intelligence. There was nothing special in his instructions, which covered the administration of the town and the work in the fields; indeed, the government of Blackland would not have seemed at all mysterious if Harry Killer had not, from time to time, bent over the ear of one of his Counsellors, to give him some confidential message whose nature Jane did not know.

The Council always lasted four hours; then everyone else went out, leaving Jane Blazon alone with Harry Killer. But soon he left her by herself. Every day, indeed, at exactly half

a

past four, he vanished beyond a little door whose key never left him. Where did he go? Of this, Jane knew absolutely nothing.

On the first three days she had waited for him to return, and a few seconds after he had gone her ear was struck by strange noises, distant cries of anguish that might be uttered by someone undergoing torture. These cries lasted about fifteen minutes; then, after being away half an hour, Harry Killer, reappearing through the little door, returned in high good humour. Jane lighted his pipes and filled his glass, whereupon he proceeded to drink himself insensible.

It was only for the three days that she awaited his return, but soon these distant cries, betokening a suffering that she was unable to relieve, so distressed her that she could bear it no longer. So she made it her custom, during her half-hour of solitude, to walk about the Palace. Soon its personnel, the Counsellors, coloured servants and the Merry Fellows on duty, began to recognize her and even to show her a certain deference.

Each evening came the moment when drunkenness left Harry Killer at her mercy. The young girl could then have got rid of him quite easily by a blow from the only legacy of her unfortunate brother, the dagger. But she had not given it. Apart from her natural reluctance to killing a defenceless man, no matter how vicious he was, what good would the murder have done? With Harry Killer dead, there would still remain the rest of that robber-band who called themselves the Counsellors, the negroes, snouted like wild beasts, who formed the Black Guard, and that horde of smugglers who composed the population of Blackland.

The position of the prisoners would not have been improved but actually worsened by the death of perhaps the only man in the whole town who, in his lucid moments, gave proof of real intelligence and could understand the advantages of mercy. Jane Blazon's companions were in full agreement with her. No, they must not slay Harry Killer at any price.

But another plan might be better. As she enjoyed the despot's confidence, might it be possible to kidnap him? Then they would have a hostage of their own, and they could meet strength with strength.

Unfortunately this plan involved great difficulties. How could they seize Harry Killer in the face of the people who moved about the Palace and the men who guarded the prisoners? Even if this difficulty were overcome, might not the people of Blackland be glad to get rid of him, and refuse to negotiate for his freedom? Finally, even if this possibility did not arise, if a peace treaty were finally arranged, how could they be certain it would be kept? To solve such problems was not easy.

In addition to this plan, Jane Blazon cherished another, which she had confided to her companions. Both her curiosity and her pity were aroused, the one by the regular absence of Harry Killer, the other by the distant cries which never failed to be heard at the same moment every evening. When Harry Killer, completely drunk, had lost consciousness, she had wished more than once to take the key of the door through which he vanished every afternoon and to see what was behind it. So far, however, her courage had failed, and she had resisted a desire whose gratification might have serious consequences.

Five days passed thus, and then came the 8th of April.

That day, a little past nine in the evening, the prisoners, including Malik, assembled on the platform of the bastion, were asking Jane Blazon about the events of the day, which had been just like its predecessor. On the floor below Tchoumouki was attending to his duties before going off until the morrow.

Although the moon was not yet in its last quarter, heavy clouds which to all appearances would not be slow in discharging themselves in rain made the night very dark. On the platform, which the lights from the other bank of the Red River did not reach, lay deep shadows.

Suddenly something fell on the paving-stones, striking them with a dull thud. The startled prisoners at once broke off their conversation. Whence had it come, and what could this thing be that their eyes could not distinguish?

Amédée Florence was the first to regain self-control. In a few moments he had discovered the mysterious projectile. It was a large pebble attached to a cord whose other end, passing across the parapet, must dip into the Red River.

What was the meaning of this? Might it not conceal a trap, or had the prisoners got, in Blackland itself, an unknown friend who wanted to send them a message? To find out, they need only pull up the cord, which might have a message attached to its end. Amédée at once began the task of hauling it in, but he had to call for the assistance of Dr. Châtonnay. Very thin, the weight it supported made it slip through their fingers. There could be no question of a mere letter.

At last they reached its end, attached to which was a much thicker cord. As they had done with the thread, they hauled it in. When they had dragged in about thirty or thirty-five yards without any difficulty, they encountered a resistance, not firm as if the cord were attached to a fixed object, but elastic, as though someone were pulling at its other end. For a few moments they felt at a loss. What were they to do?

"Fasten the cord," Amédée Florence suggested. "We shall soon see if that's what he wanted—whoever it was sent us the cord."

This was done.

At once the cord grew taut. Somebody must be climbing up it, and the prisoners, peering over the parapet, strove to catch a glimpse of him. Soon they could make out a human figure rapidly ascending the wall.

The unknown visitor completed his climb. A moment later he had scrambled over the parapet, and fell into the midst of the amazed prisoners.

Carefully keeping their voices low, they exclaimed, "Tongané!"

CHAPTER V

A NEW PRISON

NOT ONLY was Tongané still alive, but as he explained later, he had not even been wounded during the surprise attack at Koubo. The searchlights had missed him; he had been able to glide unperceived among the trees and the attackers had not troubled about him.

But he had no intention of forsaking his masters, not less because Malik was with them. He had indeed thought of trying to help them, but he had correctly decided that he could do so better if he kept his freedom.

Far from taking flight, he had followed the raiders. At the cost of endless privations while crossing the desert, he had trailed the ones who were taking Malik to Blackland. Meantime he had lived on little more than the fragments he picked up at the spots where they halted. Though on foot, he had travelled as fast as their horses, and every day he covered about thirty miles.

He did not let himself be outdistanced until they were very near Blackland. As soon as they reached the cultivated land he had stopped and had waited until nightfall before risking himself in that unknown country. Until daybreak he had hidden in the thickets. Then, mingling with the crowd of negroes, with them he had tilled the ground, with them he had received the blows of which the guards were not sparing, and with them he had gone in the evening into the central section of the city, without anyone paying any attention to him.

A few days had passed until he had found the rope in a disused hut. By its aid he had succeeded in following the Civil Body and gaining the river-bank, where for two long days he had hidden in the mouth of a sewer, waiting for a favourable opportunity.

Meanwhile he had seen the prisoners coming and going every evening on the platform of the bastion, but he had

vainly tried to attract their attention. The chance he waited
for had not come until the third day, the 8th April. Then, the
night being darkened by thick clouds, he had taken the opportunity to emerge from his dungeon and to throw to his masters
the cord which had at last enabled him to join them.

As might be supposed, he did not give this explanation until
later. For the moment he contented himself with suggesting
that they could all escape by the same method as he had
arrived. Below they would find a boat he had managed to get
hold of, and all they would have to do then would be to row
down the Red River.

Needless to say, this plan was adopted without discussion.
With four men at the oars and aided by the current, they
should make six miles an hour. If they set out before eleven,
they would have gone about forty-five miles by dawn. Thus
they would have not only got out of range of the cycloscope,
whose watch they would doubtless be able to escape by keeping in the shelter of the banks, but also beyond the cultivated
land and even beyond the last of the posts set up in the desert.
It would then be enough, so as not to be seen from the heliplanes, to hide in some irregularity of the river-banks during
the day and to resume navigation in the night, until they
should reach the Niger. The Red River must enter this near
Bikini, a village above Saye, as it followed the former bed of
the Oued Tafasasset. It was only a question, then, of a voyage
of about 280 miles all told, which would mean four or five
nights' travel.

Quickly discussed, this plan was soon adopted. First, however, they had to get rid of Tchoumouki, who sometimes used
to hang about during the evening on the gallery or the platform. They could not wait his good pleasure. They had to
act, and to act quickly.

Leaving Jane Blazon, the useless M. Poncin, and Tongané
on the top of the bastion, the other prisoners descended the
stair. From the upper steps they could see Tchoumouki on the
floor below; he was finishing his day's work with calculated

slowness. He took no notice of their presence, for he had no reason to be suspicious of them, so they could close on him without attracting his attention.

As had been arranged, it was St. Bérain who opened the attack. His sinewy hands suddenly gripped the rascal's neck, without giving him time to utter a cry. The three others then seized the negro by the arms and legs and bound him securely and gagged him. They finally thrust him into a cell, locked it, and threw the key into the Red River. Thus they delayed as much as thy could the discovery of their escape.

When, their work done, they regained the platform, the four Europeans were smitten by a flood of rain. As they had foreseen, the thick clouds dissolved in water, and the cataracts as they fell from the sky were driven along by violent squalls. Chance was certainly favouring the fugitives. Visibility was limited to twenty yards away by the liquid screen, and the lights on the far side of the river, in the Merry Fellows' quarter, could hardly be distinguished.

The descent began at once and was effected without incident. One after another, with Amédée Florence first and Tongané last, the fugitives let themselves slip down the rope; its lower end was secured to a boat large enough to hold them all. In vain it was suggested that Jane Blazon should be lowered on the end of the rope; she firmly refused, and showed that her skill and activity were equal to those of her comrades.

Before leaving the platform, Tongané took care to untie the rope. Then he simply hung it over one of the crenelations on the platform, grasped both its halves and slid down it. When he had pulled the rope down after him, there was no trace of the method by which the prisoners had escaped.

A little after ten the moorings were cast off, and the boat was carried downstream by the current. The fugitives hid behind the sides of the boat, crouched down on its floorboards. When they were beyond the town, whose outer wall was hardly six hundred yards away, they seized the oars, and their speed increased. So far, although the rain formed an almost opaque curtain, it was better to have it conceal them than for them to see where they were going.

Some minutes elapsed, and they imagined themselves outside the precincts of the town, when the boat suddenly hit against some obstacle and was held motionless. Feeling around, the fugitives realized with despair that they had been halted by an iron grille towering high above them, covered with sheet-iron plates in its upper part and with its base disappearing below the water. In vain they hauled themselves along it : its ends were fastened securely to the outer wall which enclosed on the one side the quarters of the Civil Body and the Merry Fellows, and on the other the circular road around the factory.

They had to realize that there was no way out.

Harry Killer had been right, and his precautions had been excellently carried out. Open during the day, the course of the Red River was barred during the night.

Some time elapsed before the fugitives regained their courage. Profoundly disheartened, they no longer felt the drenching rain, and were soaked to the skin without realizing it. To go back, to eat humble pie at the Palace door, and to hold out their hands to be shackled? They could never submit to that. Yet what could they do? To climb those iron plates which offered no hand-holes was plainly impossible, and still less could they dream of hauling their boat over them. But without a boat flight was impossible. As to setting foot on either of the river banks, to the left there was the Factory and to the right the Merry Fellows. On all sides the routes were closed.

"We're not going to sleep here, I suppose," Amédée Florence said at last.

"Where you want us to go?" asked Barsac, completely at a loss.

"It doesn't matter where, except to His Majesty Harry Killer," the reporter answered. "As we haven't too much to choose from, why shouldn't we try to rent a new lodging in that building which seems to be called the Factory?"

At any rate, it was worth trying. Perhaps, in that microcosm so different from the rest of the town, they might find help. As whatever happened the position could not be worse, they would risk nothing by trying.

They hauled themselves towards the left bank, and a little upstream they came to its junction with the road, about fifty yards wide, which encircled the factory. So heavy had the rain become that even at that distance they could see nothing.

Although the battle of the unchained elements dominated all other sounds as much as the swirling rain-drops limited the view, they moved very carefully along this road.

Half-way along they stopped.

They could just distinguish, twenty yards away at most, the angle formed by the western and northern walls of the Factory, the one coming in from the right parallel to the boundary of the town, and the other extending up-stream along the river bank. Unlike the façade of the Palace on that side, this part of the wall did not lead directly into the water but was separated from it by a broad quay.

Now the fugitives could not decide which way to go. They had made out, just at the very corner of the Factory, something very disquieting : a sentry-box whose classical lines could be vaguely distinguished through the rain. And a sentry-box implied a sentinel; if they did not see him it was because he had taken refuge in it.

However, they could not wait there all night. That would be the best way of being taken by surprise if the rain suddenly stopped and the suppositious sentinel were to leave his shelter.

Signing to his companions to follow, Amédée Florence retreated several paces from the Red River, then crossed the road and came back along its other side, keeping by the Factory wall. Then they could approach the sentry-box from behind, as its opening was presumably towards the riverbank.

Arrived at the corner, they paused to consider their next step; then Amédée Florence, St. Bérain and Tongané turned the corner, reached the quay, and dashed up and into the sentry-box.

A man, one of the Merry Fellows, was certainly there. Taken unawares by this unexpected attack which he had no reason to suspect, he had no chance to use his weapons, and the cry he uttered was lost in the storm. St. Bérain simply took him by the throat and hurled him to the ground, as he had hurled Tchoumouki, and the white man crumpled up just as the negro had.

Tongané ran to the boat and brought the cord, with which the Merry Fellow was securely bound. Then without waiting, the fugitives proceeded up-stream towards the Palace, filing one behind another along the Factory wall.

One of the peculiarities of the Factory was an absence, so far complete, of exterior openings. On the Esplanade side there were none, as they had seen from the top of the bastion. On the opposite side none were visible, so far as visibility was possible through the thick curtain of rain. And it now seemed that there were none in the northern façade which gave upon the river.

As, however, a quay had been built, it must be used for something. For what purpose could it have except to unload goods brought by boat? So there must necessarily be some means or other of taking them into the Factory.

Their reasoning was correct. After traversing about a hundred and fifty yards the fugitives found a large door, apparently made of sheets of iron as firm and as thick as armour-plating. How could they open this door, to which there was no exterior fastening? How could they break it down? How could they even attract the attention of the inmates without at the same time attracting that of the other sentries who in all probability were mounting guard nearby?

By the side of the great door, a few paces up-stream, there was another, similarly built but much smaller, and securely locked. Failing a key, or of anything which could be used to pick it, this was not of very much help.

After a long pause, the fugitives were on the point of deciding to hammer at the door with their fists, or if need be with their feet, when a shadow approached from up-stream, along the Esplanade. Vague in the torrential rain, the shadow came towards them. As the quay had no other exit than into the circular road along which came this nocturnal wanderer, he was likely to be making for one of the doors opening on the quay.

Having no time to move away, the fugitives huddled as best they could under the eaves of the larger door, ready to leap out upon the new-comer at the first opportunity.

But he came along so unsuspiciously, and came so close to them, almost near enough to touch them, while showing so complete an ignorance of their presence, that they abstained from any act of violence whose necessity was not clear.

Emboldened by the amazing blindness of the wanderer, they followed one by one in his footsteps, as he passed each of them in turn. When he stopped as they had foreseen in front of the smaller of the two doors, and put his key into the lock, he had behind him, ranged in a semi-circle, eight watchful spectators whose existence he did not even suspect.

The door opened. Brusquely jostling aside the man who had opened it, the fugitives dashed in after him. The last-comer closed the door, which swung to heavily.

They then found themselves in profound darkness. From this came a gentle voice which uttered, in tones of mild surprise, exclamations amazing in their moderations : "Well . . ." said the voice. "What's the meaning of this ? . . . What do you want ? . . . What's happening ?"

There suddenly gleamed a light which though feeble seemed dazzling in the darkness. Jane Blazon had thought of switching on her electric torch which had already rendered a signal service at Kokoro. Its beam at once revealed Tongané and, facing him, a slender man, with light fair hair, his clothes dripping water, and a little out of breath, who was leaning against the wall.

As soon as they saw each other Tongané and the fair man exclaimed simultaneously, though in very different tones :

"Sergeant Tongané!" said the latter, with the same gentle voice and in the same accent of mild surprise.

"Massa Camaret!" cried the negro, rolling his frightened eyes.

Camaret! . . . Jane Blazon shuddered on hearing that name; she knew it well, for it was the name of one of her brother's former comrades.

However, Amédée Florence thought it time to intervene. Among people who know one another there's no need for introductions. He took a pace forward into the cone of light.

"Monsieur Camaret," he said, "my friends and I would like a word with you."

"Nothing simpler," replied Camaret calmly.

He pressed a button, and electric lights shone out in the ceiling. The fugitives realized that they were in a vaulted room devoid of any article of furniture. Some sort of entrance hall, apparently.

Marcel Camaret opened a door behind which was a stairway. Then, politely standing a little aside : "If you will be good enough to come in," he said quite simply.

CHAPTER VI

MARCEL CAMARET

ASTOUNDED by this welcome, whose banal courtesy seemed extraordinary in such circumstances, the six Europeans, followed by the two negroes, went up the stairs, which were brilliantly lit by electric lamps. After climbing twenty steps, they entered a second hall, where they stopped. Coming up behind them, Marcel Camaret went through the hall, opened another door, and stood aside as before to allow his unexpected guests to precede him.

They entered an immense room completely in disorder. A great draughtsman's table stood against one wall, and bookcases against the three others. A dozen or so chairs were scattered at random, all piled up with books and papers. Marcel Camaret picked up one of these piles, placed it quietly on the floor, and sat down. Encouraged by this example, his guests copied him, and soon—except for Malik and Tongané, who remained respectfully standing—they were all seated.

"How can I help you?" asked Marcel Camaret, who seemed to regard this unexpected visit as the most natural thing in the world.

During the few minutes which it took them to settle down, the fugitives had had time to inspect the person whose home they had so unceremoniously entered, and that inspection had not failed to reassure them. Certainly he was strange enough, this person whom Tongané had greeted by the name of Camaret; who had been so deeply wrapped in thought that he had brushed against them on the quay without so much as seeing them; whose other-worldly air seemed to place him above mundane affairs; whose calm simplicity as he welcomed those who burst in on him so unceremoniously, had been extraordinary; this was not to be denied.

But these details, unusual though they were, did not conflict with the honesty, to be more precise with the "innocence," so

77

plainly shown by this man, whose body, as yet not fully formed, resembled that of an adolescent. No, the owner of that broad and well-shaped forehead and the clear glance of those splendid eyes could not belong to the same moral family as Harry Killer, although everything indicated that they shared the same life.

"Monsieur Camaret," said Barsac, who had regained his confidence, "we have come to ask you for protection."

"For protection . . ." Camaret repeated, with a slight air of surprise. "Against whom, in Heaven's name?"

"Against the master—or rather the despot—of this town : against Harry Killer."

"Harry Killer! . . . A despot! . . ." Camaret repeated once more; he did not seem able to understand.

"You didn't know this?" asked Barsac, no less surprised.

"No, indeed."

"You must realize, though, that there's a town here?" Barsac insisted, a little impatiently.

"Of course!" Camaret agreed.

"Isn't this town called Blackland?"

"Oh, then it's Blackland that it's called?" mused Camaret. "That's not at all a bad name. . . . No, I didn't know that, but I know it now you've told me. Not that I care about it."

"If you didn't know the name of the town," continued Barsac, not without a certain irony, "you knew, I suppose, that it's inhabited, and that it's got a fairly large population?"

"Naturally," replied Camaret quietly.

"Well, any town must have some sort of administration, a government."

"Naturally."

"In Blackland, the government is completely in the hands of Harry Killer. And he's nothing but a rogue, a cruel and bloodthirsty despot, a drunken brute, not to say a lunatic."

Marcel Camaret lifted towards Barsac the eyes which he had hitherto lowered. He seemed lost, completely bewildered, and looked almost as if he had dropped out of the moon.

"Oh, oh," he murmured, confusedly. "You're using language. . . ."

"Which is quite inadequate considering the facts behind them," Barsac continued; he was beginning to get annoyed. "But first let me explain who we are."

Camaret having assented by a gesture of polite indifference which was hardly encouraging, he performed the introductions. Leaving Jane Blazon the pseudonym she had chosen, he indicated in turn his companions and himself, adding after each name the quality of the person in question.

"And finally," he concluded, "this is Tongané, whom I needn't stress; it seems you know him already."

"Yes . . . yes . . ." said Camaret mildly, once more looking down.

"Instructed by the French Government. . . . But surely you are a Frenchman, Monsieur Camaret?"

"Yes . . . yes," murmured the engineer, again in tones devoid of emotion.

"Instructed, as I said, by the French Government to carry out in the Niger Bend a mission in which my companions here were taking part," Barsac continued, "we have had unending struggles against the obstacles which it pleased Harry Killer to place in our way."

"Why should he do that?" Camaret objected, at last showing signs of attention.

"So as to keep us from reaching the Niger, for Harry Killer means his lair to stay unknown. That's why he endeavoured to bar us out from the region—for fear that we should hear about Blackland : there's nobody in Europe who so much as suspects that it exists."

"What's that you say?" cried Camaret, with an unusual show of interest. "But they can't help knowing it exists! Not in Europe, where so many workmen have gone after they left here."

"It is so, none the less," Barsac replied.

"You mean to tell me," Camaret insisted : he was getting

more and more anxious, "that nobody—I say nobody—knows about us?"

"Nobody whatever."

"And they still think that this part of the desert is quite uninhabited?"

"Yes, Monsieur, I do say so."

Camaret had risen. Gripped by a powerful emotion, he walked up and down the room.

"Unthinkable! . . . Unthinkable! . . ." he murmured.

His agitation lasted only a few minutes. Soon, having regained his calm by an effort of the will, he again seated himself. "Go on, Monsieur, I implore you," he said; he had turned paler than usual.

"I won't weary you," Barsac continued, in response to this invitation, "by telling you all the troubles we have had to face. It's quite enough to say that, after he had succeeded in robbing us of our escort, Harry Killer grew furious at seeing that we kept on in the direction he had forbidden. So at last he had us pounced on by his men in the depths of night, and brought us here. And now he's kept us prisoner for fourteen days, and threatens us with the rope."

A little blood had risen to the face of Marcel Camaret, which had begun to put on a menacing look.

"What you say is unthinkable!" he cried, when M. Barsac had finished. What! . . . Harry Killer to have acted like that!"

"That isn't everything"—and Barsac went on to describe the odious violence to which Jane Blazon had been subjected and the slaughter of the two negroes, one wiped out by an aerial torpedo and the other pounced on by heliplane and dropped on to the tower platform, on which he had been hideously smashed.

Marcel Camaret was in consternation. For the first time, perhaps, he left the realm of pure abstract thought to come to grips with reality. His innate honesty was suffering badly from the contact. What—he who would not have crushed an insect—he had, without suspecting anything, lived for long years in association with a being capable of such atrocities!

"It's horrible! . . . frightful! . . ." he said.

The horror with which this narration had inspired him was obviously as sincere as it was deep. How could he reconcile his conscience, his deep moral rectitude, with his presence in a town rendered suspicious by the character of its chief?

"But now, Monsieur," Barsac suggested, putting the general thought into words, "a man who can commit such acts in cold blood is no amateur. Harry Killer must certainly have other crimes on his conscience. You don't know of any?"

"You—you dare to ask me such a question?" Camaret protested in disgust. "Yes, certainly, I didn't know of them, just as I didn't know about the ones you've now told me, as well as others, more terrible still, that I'm beginning to suspect. Hardly ever coming out of this factory where so much depends upon me, busy thinking out new schemes, I can certainly say that I've never seen anything, never known anything—never, never."   ,

"If you understand us well enough," said Barsac, "you will be able to give the answer, partly at any rate, to a question which we asked ourselves as soon as we got here. We are amazed that this town and the adjoining countryside can be the work of a Harry Killer. When we remember that ten years ago it was nothing but a sea of sand! Whatever its purpose, the change is amazing. And even if Harry Killer used to be endowed with real intelligence, that intelligence has long been drowned in alcohol. We don't at all see how such a degenerate can have achieved such wonders."

"Him! . . ." exclaimed Marcel Camaret, gripped by a sudden anger. "Him! . . . That nobody, that nonentity! What are you thinking of! . . . The work is good, and to carry it out needed someone very different from Harry Killer."

"Then who's responsible for it," asked Barsac.

"I am!" came the superb words of Camaret, his face shining with pride. "It was I who created everything that exists round here. It was I who showered the life-giving rain on the scorched arid surface of the desert. It was I who transformed it into a flourishing and fertile countryside. It was I who made this town out of nothing just as God created the Universe out of the void!"

Barsac and his companions exchanged uneasy glances. While, trembling with a sickly enthusiasm, he had sung that hymn to his own glory, Marcel Camaret had raised his rolling eyes heavenwards, as if he were looking for someone to compare himself with. Mightn't they have gone from one madman to another?

"Well," asked Dr. Châtonnay after a moment's silence, "as it was you who originated everything we have seen here, how could you hand over your work to Harry Killer without troubling what use he was making of it?"

"When He launched the stars into infinity," replied Camaret proudly, "did it trouble the Eternal Power what would become of them?"

"He has been known to punish," the doctor murmured.

"And I will punish as He does, if need be," declared Marcel Camaret, whose eyes were again gleaming with that disquieting light.

The fugitives were at a loss. How could they rely on this man, maybe a genius but certainly unbalanced, capable at once of so total a blindness and so unmeasured a pride?

"Would it be indiscreet, Monsieur Camaret," said Amédée Florence, who wanted to bring the conversation back to more immediate ends, "if I were to ask you how you got to know Harry Killer, and how the plan for creating Blackland came into your head?"

"Not at all," replied Marcel Camaret gently; he was gradually regaining his usual calm. "The idea came from Harry Killer, but its execution was left to me. I knew him when I took part in an expedition organized by an English Company and led by a captain seconded from military duty, a captain called George Blazon."

At that name all eyes were directed on Jane. But she remained unmoved.

"Tongané took part in that expedition in the rank of a sergeant," Camaret went on, "and that's why I recognized him just now in spite of the years which have elapsed. As to myself, I had been engaged as an engineer, my task being to study the orography, the hydrography, and especially the mineralogy of the regions we crossed. Setting out from Acera, in Ashanti-land, we had travelled northwards for two months when one day Harry Killer turned up among us. Heartily welcomed by our leader, he joined our column and never left it."

"Wouldn't it be right to say," Jane asked, "that at last he assumed Captain Blazon's place so gradually that nobody noticed it?"

Camaret turned towards the young girl. "I couldn't tell you," he said, hesitating a little but showing no signs of surprise at the question. "I was so busy with my own work, you will understand, that I couldn't notice any details, and I saw Harry Killer little more than I saw George Blazon. However, that may be, when I got back one day from a personal expedition of forty-eight hours I couldn't find the column where I had left it. No men, no equipment, nothing! Much annoyed, I must admit, I was wondering what direction to follow when I met Harry Killer.

"He told me that Captain Blazon had gone back to the coast with most of the personnel and that it was left to him, with about twenty men and myself, to complete the itinerary. What did it matter to me, he or Captain Blazon—especially as I did not know where to find him? So I followed Harry Killer without hesitation. He had heard rumours about some fairly interesting inventions which I then had in mind. He brought me here and suggested that I should implement them. I agreed. That was the beginning of my relations with Harry Killer."

"Monsieur Camaret, you must allow me to complete your

information about Harry Killer, and to tell you what you don't seem to know," said Jane Blazon in serious tones. "From the day when he joined Captain Blazon's expedition, the column which he commanded became a horde of bandits. It burned the villages, massacred very many men, ripped up the women, and hacked the children to pieces."

"Impossible! . . . Camaret protested. "Devil take it, I was there! And I didn't see anything."

"Just as you haven't seen anything recently although it was in front of you, just as for the last ten years you've known nothing about the acts of Harry Killer. Alas, the events I've described cannot be denied; they are historic facts which all the world knows."

"And I knew nothing of it! . . ." babbled Marcel Camaret thunderstruck.

"However that may be," Jane Blazon continued, "the rumour of these atrocities reached Europe. The troops were sent against Captain Blazon's rebel column and it was destroyed. On that day when you failed to find anyone at the camp you had left, George Blazon had not moved away from it. He was dead."

"Dead!" repeated Camaret, astonished.

"Yes, but he hadn't been struck, as everyone thought until recently, by the bullets of the troops sent after him. George Blazon had been assassinated."

"Assassinated. . . ."

"You were misinformed just now. My name is not Mornas. I am Jane Blazon, and I was the sister of your former leader. That's why I recognized your name as soon as Tongané uttered it. The only reason I came into Africa was to find a proof of my poor brother's innocence, accused of crimes which were undoubtedly committed by someone else."

"Assassinated! . . ." repeated Camaret, borne down by the weight of this series of revelations.

"And murdered from behind," Jane added, producing the weapon by which George Blazon had been killed. "Along with these gentlemen, I went to my brother's grave, and there, in their presence, I exhumed his remains. We found this dagger which had pierced through the shoulder-blade that still held it firmly and which had reached his heart. The murderer's name had been engraved on the hilt, but unfortunately time has effaced it. But there are still two letters showing, and from what you have told us, I don't think I'm mistaken in saying that this name must be 'Harry Killer'."

While listening to this tragic history, Marcel Camaret had shown a growing agitation. He was writhing his fingers restlessly together and passing his hands over his face, on which drops of sweat were glistening.

"It's terrible! . . . Terrible! That I should have done this! . . . I! . ." he kept repeating, while a troubled light gleamed anew in his dilated eyes.

"You'll let us hide here?" asked Barsac by way of summing things up.

"Will I let you hide! . . ." replied Camaret with unaccustomed heat. "Need you ask? Can you imagine that I'm a part to these abominable crimes which on the contrary you can be sure I mean to punish!"

"Before talking about punishing, we have to think about protecting ourselves," remarked the ever-practical Amédée Florence. "Won't we have to fear that Harry Killer will try to recapture us?"

Marcel Camaret smiled. "He doesn't know you're here," he said, "and even if he did . . ." a gesture showed how little he cared about that. "For the time being," he continued, "you can set your minds at ease. You're quite safe here, you can be sure of that."

He pressed a button and a bell rang. A black servant appeared. "Jacko," Camaret said, as though it were the simplest thing in the world, while the negro rolled his startled eyes. "Show these gentlemen and this lady to their rooms."

He rose, crossed the room, and opened a door. "Good evening, gentlemen," he said politely. Then he vanished, leaving his guests as astonished as the negro, upon whom had devolved the difficult task of finding them beds.

Where, indeed, could poor Jacko have found them. There were none free in the Factory, and no provision had been made for unexpected arrivals. Would he have to go from door to door and arouse the workmen one after another?

Realizing the difficulty, Barsac assured him that he and his companions could do without beds. They would stay where they were, and they merely asked Jacko to get them all he could in the way of arm-chairs and wraps. They would manage quite well, especially as the night was so far advanced.

At last came daybreak. At exactly six o'clock Marcel Camaret opened the door by which he had gone out. He did not seem at all surprised to find his room converted into a dormitory.

"Good morning, gentlemen," he said to his guests, as calmly as he had previously wished them good night.

"Good morning, Monsieur Camaret," they replied with one voice.

"Gentlemen," Camaret continued, "I have thought over what you told me last night. This situation cannot continue. We must act at once."

He touched a button. At once a noisy clanging resounded from all sides.

"Kindly follow me, gentlemen," he said.

After traversing several corridors they reached a huge workshop equipped with a number of machines, now motionless. Around them assembled a crowd of men and women.

"Everybody here?" asked Camaret. "Rigaud, please call the roll."

Having ascertained that the personnel of the Factory were all present, he addressed them. He first introduced the strangers who had come to claim his protection. Then he made clear what he had learned during the night.

Atrocities committed by George Blazon's men after for some

reason or other they had come under the control of Harry
Killer; the murder plainly attributable to the latter; the kidnapping and internment of the Barsac Mission; the violence
offered to Jane Blazon; and finally the slaughter, as cruel as it
was unjustified, of the two negroes—he forgot nothing which
could impress the minds of his audience.

This made it clear that they were all of them unwittingly in
the service of an out-and-out bandit and gave them reason to
fear that the work of the Factory would serve for promoting
further crimes. Such a situation could not be allowed to continue, and honour forbade them to surrender the prisoners
whom Harry Killer was illegally detaining. Thence it followed
that they must break off all negotiations with the Palace and,
one and all, demand to be repatriated.

Heard in complete silence, the narration of Camaret first
aroused a very natural amazement among these honest workmen. When they had regained their calm, they fully agreed
with his conclusions. Which of them, indeed, would have
thought of expressing an opinion contrary to that of the
Director whom they all admired and respected?

He had finally struck the imagination of his auditors in explaining the conclusion he had reached: "What has most
surprised me," he said, "of all the incredible things which I
learned that night, is that nobody in Europe has heard of the
existence of this town which Harry Killer seems to call Blackland. I am not ignorant that it was founded, far from any
caravan route, in the heart of the desert where nobody ever
comes—and for a very good reason.

"But it is no less certain that a number of our comrades,
after having been here some time, have been smitten with
home-sickness and wanted to go back. I counted them up last
night. Since we began, a hundred and thirty-seven have left
us. Now if only a few of these had arrived in Europe, the
existence of this town could no longer be unknown. As nobody
has heard of it, we can only infer that none of the hundred
and thirty-seven have ever reached their destination."

Not a sound was heard from the assembled workmen, who seemed thunderstruck by this irrefutable argument.

"And the result of that," Camaret ended, "is that not one of you can ever hope to see his homeland again, so long as the power of Harry Killer exists, and that we must not expect any mercy if we fall into his hands. In our own interests, as well as in that of justice, we must revolt."

"Yes! . . . yes! . . . You can rely on us!" came the shouts from every side.

Such was their confidence in Marcel Camaret that these workmen, at first dispirited at finding themselves cut off from the rest of the world, had already regained their courage on remembering that he was with them. All arms were stretched towards him as a sign of unshakable fidelity.

"Let the work go on as usual and rely on me," he said, going out to the accompaniment of a storm of cheers.

As soon as he left the workshop he spent a few moments with his foreman, whom he had addressed as Rigaud. Then, while the latter went off to carry out his orders, Camaret returned to his study, his protegés following him.

Scarcely had they entered when the telephone-bell rang. He grasped the receiver, and the others heard him replying in his gentle voice: "yes" or "no", "good" or "As you wish", to the messages he received. Finally he began laughing and replaced the receiver, shutting it off by means of a cut-out in the circuit.

"That was Harry Killer telephoning me," he said, in that remarkable voice whose gentle mildness was scarcely affected by any emotion. "He knows you are here."

"Already!" exclaimed Barsac.

"Yes. He seems to have found someone called Tchoumouki. They have also found a boat abandoned in the river and an official tied up like Tchoumouki. As to leave the town at night is impossible without his knowing it, he has inferred that you must be here. I did not deny it. He then asked me to hand you over. I refused. He insisted, and I reiterated my refusal.

This aroused his wrath. He threatened to come and take you by force. That made me smile, and I broke off the conversation."

The others had risen with a single movement.

"There's no need to say that you can rely on us," Barsac declared on behalf of them all. "But we must have weapons. . . ."

"Weapons? . . ." Camaret repeated with a smile. "What for? . . . I don't think there's even one of them here. None the less, you need not be uneasy, gentlemen. We can use other methods."

"Methods able to resist the Palace guns?"

"Those and many other things. If it occurred to me to destroy the whole town, I could do it in an instant. But I hardly think we shall be reduced to that extremity. The Palace guns will remain silent, be assured of that.

"Not only does Killer realize my power, and realize, too, that most of the Factory is shell-proof, he will take care not to destroy it, for he knows that his whole power is based on it. He's more likely to try to get in with living agents. But he will not succeed."

As though in response to his declaration, they heard heavy blows coming from the floor beneath.

"What did I tell you?" said the engineer, smiling gently. "There they are, attacking the door. But I can guarantee that it's solidly built."

"But if they bring a cannon to bear on it?" asked Barsac, only half reassured by the engineer's calm.

"Even so it would not be easy to break it down," replied the latter. "But to bring one of the palace guns on to the quay, that would take time, and we've only got to deal with a battering-ram wielded by human arms. Using that, they could batter for a century without getting any further. Still, if you care to come with me, you can be present at the edge of the siege. I think the sight will interest you."

They went back to the workshop and crossed it without stopping. The machines were in action now, but the men were not showing their usual zeal. Grouped together, they were discussing the news they had heard, and the place showed a certain disorder easily explicable in the light of recent events, and to which Camaret closed his eyes.

Having crossed the workshop, they climbed a spiral staircase and reached the platform of a tower; the only difference between this and that of the Palace was that it was surmounted by that inexplicable metal pylon whose tip rose more than a hundred yards into the air. Like the Palace tower, too, it was provided with a cycloscope placed between the supports of the pylon; Camaret asked his companions to enter this.

"This cycloscope," he explained, "does not cover a range of several miles like the one I built for Harry Killer. Thanks to a series of mirrors placed obliquely along the top of the Factory wall, we can observe what happens in our immediate vicinity. From here you can see the outer face of the surrounding wall right down to its foot."

The Esplanade, the quay, and the circular road were indeed visible in the cycloscope whose images, though much smaller than those of the Palace instrument, were much clearer. Through the lenses they saw a number of men, several carrying ladders, running all round the Factory wall, while about thirty others were still exhausting themselves in fruitless efforts against the door.

"As I foresaw," said Camaret. "They're going to launch an attack. Now this should really begin to get interesting."

The attack was certainly beginning. Already several ladders had been reared against the wall, and on these were a number of the Merry Fellows. Reaching its crest, several of them grasped it unsuspiciously.

The scene changed at once. Scarcely had they touched the top of the wall when these men exhibited the most frightful contortions. Hanging from the crest, as though their arms were glued to the wall, they danced the devil of a jig, like jumping-jacks when someone pulls the strings.

"That's stupid of them," explained Camaret. "The edge of the wall is completely covered with a metal which I invented, a hundred times as good a conductor as copper. I sent an alternating current of suitable voltage through it and you see the result."

While he was giving that explanation, the attackers on the lower ladders had seized the legs of the men above them, whose frantic movements they could not understand. At once these reckless fellows performed the same antics, to the complete bewilderment of their companions who had not followed their example.

"But why don't those lunatics simply let themselves drop off?" asked St. Bérain.

"They can't, the poor devils," Marcel Camaret explained. "They'll stop fixed to the wall as long as I wish. . . . But I can do even better."

He grasped a switch. At that moment the ladders were overthrown, as though thrust back by an invisible hand, and the men who had been holding them tumbled pell-mell, leaving on the wall only those human bunches of grapes who were fastened to it and who continued to struggle desperately.

"I won't be responsible for any damage," remarked Camaret gently. "This has happened under your eyes—would you like to know how it was done?"

When they all agreed, he continued :

"It's quite simple. In my opinion force, whatever its nature, consists of nothing but different kinds of vibrations in the ether. It is generally agreed that light can be considered as a series of vibrations between certain limits of frequency, and that electrical phenomena are a different series of vibrations separated from the first by an interval supposed to appertain to other vibrations whose nature is unknown. Without finally deciding, I incline to believe that these last have some relation with heat. However this may be, I know how to produce them and use them to obtain somewhat strange results, like those of which I have just given you proof."

During this brief explanation, the human grapes continued their fantastic dance.

"That little game has lasted long enough," he said, throwing over another switch.

At once the human jumping-jacks dropped off the walls and fell thirty feet to its base, where they remained motionless. After a moment of understandable hesitation, their comrades decided to come and carry them off.

"End of the first act," Camaret announced in his usual voice. "I don't think it's ended to Harry Killer's benefit; already about thirty of his men are out of action. Suppose we next deal with the lunatics who so stupidly persist in clamouring at the door?"

He seized a telephone transmitter. "Are you ready, Rigaud?" he asked.

"Yes, Sir," replied a voice audible everywhere in the cycloscope.

"Send!" ordered Camaret.

As if in direct obedience to his order, a strange-looking implement at once emerged and moved away from the base of the tower. It was some sort of vertical cylinder, the end facing the ground expanded to form a large cone.

At the other end four screws, one horizontal and three vertical, spun with dazzling speed. This strange contrivance soared into the air, moving away from the exterior wall. When it was several yards high, its course became horizontal, and it rigorously followed the Factory boundary.

But already, following this first contrivance, had come a second, then a third, then others. Camaret's guests could count twenty which, at regular intervals, left the tower like birds leaving the nest and in turn completed the same manœuvre.

"Those are my 'wasps'," said Marcel Camaret, slightly stressing the possessive pronoun. "I'll explain later how they are steered. For the time being, just watch them at work."

Again he lifted the telephone transmitter. "A warning, Rigaud," he said.

Then, speaking to his new friends, "After all, why should I kill those poor devils who've done nothing to me? A warning will do, if they're willing to accept it."

Since their attempt had been halted, the attackers who had tried to scale the wall had stayed motionless. Carrying away their comrades who were out of action—several had certainly been killed or at least badly injured—they had evacuated the circular road and had gathered together on the Esplanade, at a respectful distance from the Factory, and were staring at its wall in bewilderment.

On the other hand those who were attacking the door had not interrupted their work. They were obstinately battering at the portal, which didn't seem to be much damaged, with a great beam which about forty strong arms were swinging. In circling the boundary, the wasps, as Marcel Camaret called them, passed one after another over this group, which paid no attention to them.

Suddenly an explosion sounded from one of the wasps, and a hail like machine-gun bullets covered the ground, over a circle about a hundred yards across.

At the noise, the men who were swinging the ram looked up. They had not yet understood what caused it when a second explosion sounded from another of the contrivances as it reached them; the explosion was followed, like the first, by a machine-gun hail.

This time the field of fire was nearer and several men were hit by the projectiles. The others did not wait. Dropping the ram, they gathered up the wounded and ran away as fast as their legs could carry them.

The onlookers could hardly believe their eyes. Each wasp, after being fired, had obediently returned into its nest at the foot of the tower. Then, having been reloaded, it set off to regain its place in the general circle.

"I don't think we need trouble about those fellows," said Marcel Camaret. "So if it would please you, by any chance, to visit the Factory. . . ."

CHAPTER VII

BLACKLAND FACTORY

HIS GUESTS were only too ready to accept.

"We shall come back here when we've finished our tour of the Factory," said Camaret, "but first notice its general layout. You see it covers a rectangular surface about 250 yards wide by about 360 yards along the river. Its area is roughly twenty acres : its western part, about three fifths of the rectangle, is devoted to gardens."

"Why gardens?" broke in Amédée Florence.

"They give us part of our food, the rest comes from outside. So it's only the remainder, about a hundred yards wide, with an entrance on the quay, which forms the Factory itself. At its centre, over a length of about 250 yards, the workshops and my own quarters are grouped at the foot of that central tower. So at each end there's a space of about 60 yards where a broad street, perpendicular to the river, separates two rows of workmen's quarters. As each row includes seven houses, and each house has four storeys, including the ground floor, we have 120 dwellings."

"What's the size of your staff?" asked Barsac.

"Exactly a hundred men, but several are married and there are some children. As you can see, the workshops are only one storey high and they are covered with a thick layer of turfed soil. So shells would be almost powerless against them. Now you know the general layout, we can go down, if you wish, and make a detailed visit."

Before accepting that invitation, Camaret's audience threw a last glance around. There was no change in the situation. The wasps were still making their circular promenade, and the attackers, rendered wise by experience, did not dare enter the zone of peril. Reassured, the party followed the engineer off the platform.

Under his leadership, they first visited the part of the tower which he called the hive, whence the twenty wasps had emerged from as many cells; between these was placed their reserve ammunition. They then traversed a series of work-rooms, the fitting-shop, mill, forge, foundry, and so forth, and emerged in the gardens, on the side nearest the Palace.

The high wall around the Factory hid this from them. But when they had gone about fifty yards from the wall, the crest of Harry Killer's tower came into sight. At once an explosion sounded from its top and was followed by the characteristic whine of a bullet passing over their heads. They recoiled hurriedly.

"The fool! . . ." Camaret murmured calmly; then, without halting, he simply raised his arm.

The sign was followed by a violent hissing. His guests instinctively turned towards the Factory, but Camaret pointed to the Palace. The cycloscope which crowned its tower had vanished.

"That will teach him," said the inventor. "I've got aerial torpedoes, too! Indeed, I've got more than he has, because I made them. As for the cycloscope, I'll build another, that's all."

"But, Monsieur," asked Amédée Florence. "As you've got these projectiles which you call aerial torpedoes, why don't you use them against Harry Killer?"

For a moment Camaret stared at the man who had asked the question, and again a bewildered look came into his eyes.

"Me! . . ." He said at last in a dull voice. "Me, to destroy my own work! . . ."

Without pressing the point, Amédée Florence exchanged a glance with his companions. With all his high qualities, this remarkable man certainly had one chink in his armour, and that chink was pride.

They walked on in silence. The Palace had learned its lesson. No other attack was made upon them as they went on through the garden.

"Now we're coming to the interesting part," said Camaret,

as he opened a door. "This used to be the power unit, the motor and steam engine and boiler which we fed with wood, for want of any other fuel. That was quite a business, for the wood came some distance, and we used a great deal of it. Fortunately that didn't last long. As soon as the river was flowing, fed by the rainfall I had produced, the hydro-electric station began to work; I had meantime built it about six miles up-stream. Now we no longer use this archaic equipment, and smoke no longer gushes from that useless chimney. We're quite satisfied to meet all our needs from the energy which the generating station sends us."

They followed Camaret into another room.

"Here," he explained, "and in the next rooms, which are filled like this with dynamos, alternators, transformers and coils, this is the realm of the thunderbolt. It is here we use and transform the main current which the station sends us."

"What?" cried Florence, amazed. "You were able to bring all these machines here?"

"Only a few of them," replied Camaret, "most of them we built ourselves."

"Still you'd have needed the raw materials," Florence objected. "How the devil did you get them in the midst of the desert?"

"Well!" said Camaret, who had paused thoughtfully as if this point were quite new to him, "you are right, Monsieur Florence. How could the first machines have come here, as well as the raw materials we used for the others? I've never considered that side of the question, I must admit. I asked for them, and I got them. I didn't look any further. But now you draw my attention to it. . . ."

"And what a sacrifice of men, to bring all that across the desert, until you had the heliplanes."

"That is true," admitted Camaret, who had turned rather pale.

"And the money? For all that must have swallowed up the cash!" Florence asked in a tone of familiar boldness.

"The money?" babbled Camaret.

"Yes, the money. Certainly you must be rich?"

"Me! . . ." Camaret protested. "I don't think I've had five centimes in my pocket since I came here."

"Then?"

"It's Harry Killer. . . ." Camaret began timidly.

"True enough, but where did he get it? Is he a millionaire, your Harry Killer?"

Camaret extended his arms in token of his ignorance. This question seemed to have demoralized him, and again his eyes took on that lost expression devoid of any living emotion. Foreseeing the possible answer to the question put to him so brusquely, a problem quite different from those he usually had to solve, he felt a sort of faintness before the unsuspected horizons which opened out before him. He seemed so completely lost that Dr. Châtonnay took pity on him.

"That's a point we can clear up later with the others," he said. "But now don't let's dwell on it all day, let's get on with our visit."

As if to drive away too pressing a thought, Camaret passed his hand over his forehead and silently entered the next room.

"Here," he said, in a voice still touched by emotion, "these are the compressors. We make much use of liquid air and other gases. As you know, every gas can be liquefied, so long as it's sufficiently compressed and the temperature is low enough, but as soon as the liquids are left to themselves, they warm up and more or less quickly regain their gaseous state. Then if they're in a closed receptacle, they exert so great a pressure on its casing that it flies into fragments.

"One of my inventions has changed all that. In fact, I have discovered a substance which is completely anti-diathermic— completely impermeable to heat. The result is that a liquefied gas—air for example—in a container made of this substance will always keep the same temperature. So it remains liquid and never has the slightest tendency to explode. This inven-

D

tion has enabled me to produce several others, notably the long-range heliplanes which you know about."

"Which we know about! . . ." exclaimed Amédée Florence. "You may say we know about them only too well! Then it was you who made them, too?"

"And who did you think made them?" asked Camaret, suddenly assailed by a new attack of his inordinate pride.

As he spoke, however, his emotion gradually vanished. Soon no trace of it remained, and he had quite regained his self-control when he continued :

"My heliplanes have three special features, their stability, their take-off, and their motive power; I will give you a brief idea of them.

"Let's begin with the stability. When a bird meets the thrust of a sudden squall, it does not need calculations to regain its equilibrium. Its nervous system—or rather what the physiologists call its reflexes—come into action and it balances quite instinctively. For the stability of my mechanical birds to be automatic, I wanted to give them a similar system of reflexes. As you have seen, they are provided with two wings placed at the top of a pylon fifteen feet high, based on the platform for the motor, the pilot, and the passengers. That arrangement results in a marked lowering of the centre of gravity.

"But the pylon is by no means fixed in relation to the wings. Unless it is securely held, by the directional or altitudinal rudders, it is free to oscillate slightly in all directions about the vertical. So if, apart from the action of the rudder, the wings dip sideways or forwards, the pylon is forced by its own weight to tend to produce a new angle with them. This movement at once brings into action weights free to slide parallel or perpendicular to the wings, which meantime are warped appropriately. This immediately—and automatically—corrects the accidental oscillations of the heliplane."

His eyes lowered towards the ground, Marcel Camaret gave this explanation with the calmness of a professor delivering a lecture. He never faltered, never groped for words, which came to him of themselves. Without a pause he continued in the same tones :

"Let us proceed to the second point. At the moment of take-off, the wings of the heliplane are lowered and furled against the pylon. At the same time the axis of the screw, free to move in a verticle plane perpendicular to the wings, rises, bringing the screw to the horizontal. The apparatus thus becomes a helicopter, and the sole function of its screw is suspensory. But, when it has reached a sufficient height, the wings open, and at the same time the axis of the screw inclines forward until it is horizontal. Gradually the screw thus becomes propulsive, and the helicopter is transformed into an airplane.

"As for the motive force, it is provided by liquid air. From a fuel-tank constructed of the anti-diathermic substance I mentioned, the liquid air, its flow regulated by a series of valves, reaches a tube which is always kept warm. The air at once returns to its gaseous state, exerts a great pressure, and actuates the motor."

"What speed do you get with these heliplanes?" asked Amédée Florence.

"Two hundred and fifty miles an hour for three thousand miles, with no need for refuelling," replied Camaret.

Nil mirari, so said Horace, don't be surprised at anything. But Camaret's hearers could not conceal their admiration. As they returned to the tower they could not find terms enthusiastic enough to praise his genius. But that strange man, who none the less sometimes showed so overweening a pride, seemed to care little for their applause, as though he valued only the praise he bestowed on himself.

"Now we are coming to the very heart of the Factory," he said when they reached the tower. "This tower includes six floors similar to this and equipped with similar apparatus. You have undoubtedly noticed that its summit is surmounted by a very tall metal pylon. This pylon is a 'wave projector'. The tower bristles, moreover, with a number of points; these are smaller projectors."

"Wave projectors, you say?" asked Dr. Châtonnay.

"I'm not going to give you a course in physics," said Marcel Camaret smilingly. "But a few explanations of its principles are however necessary. I will remind you, then, if you know it already, or tell you, if you don't, that a celebrated German physicist called Hertz noticed some time ago that when an electric spark from an induction coil flashes across a short gap between the two terminals of a condenser—or a resonator or oscillator, whichever word pleases you best—that spark sets up between the two poles of the instrument an oscillating discharge.

"The gap is crossed by an alternating current, or, in other words, the two poles are alternatively positive and negative throughout the one discharge, until this returns to a state of equilibrium. The speed of these oscillations, also known as their frequency, can be very great, as much as a hundred thousand million a second.

"Now these oscillations are not limited to the points which produce them. On the other hand they set up a disturbance in their surroundings, the air—or, more precisely, in the imponderable fluid which at once fills interstellar space and the intermolecular interstices of material bodies, and which is called the ether.

"To each oscillation there thus corresponds an etheric vibration which by degrees is transmitted ever further away. These vibrations are rightly called the Hertzian Waves. Have I made myself clear?"

"Admirably," replied Barsac, who, as a politician, was perhaps of all Camaret's hearers the least prepared for scientific questions.

"Except for myself," the scientist continued, "these waves were only a laboratory curiosity. They were used to electrify, without any material contact, metallic bodies at varying distances from their point of emission. They had the overwhelming defect of spreading in all directions round that point, exactly like the concentric circles formed in a pool when a stone is dropped into it. The result is that their initial energy is diluted, weakened, dissipated, so to speak, in spreading over an ever-increasing space. So that, at only a few yards from their source, nothing more than insignificant reactions can be obtained. Do you still understand? I am quite clear?"

"Luminously," declared Amédée Florence.

"Again except for myself, though it had been noticed that these waves can be reflected like light, nobody had ever drawn any conclusion from this. But, thanks to a metal of super-conductivity which I have discovered—the very same with which I have garnished the crest of our wall—I have been able to construct reflectors which enable the whole strength of the waves to be concentrated in any direction I wish.

"Their original strength can thus be completely transmitted in any direction through space, because it has not been ex-pended in any sort of work. Methods of varying the frequency of these oscillations being well known, I was able to think up receivers for the waves which would respond solely to an assigned frequency. This is what physicists call 'syntonization'!

"A receiver can thus be constructed only to react to all the waves having the frequencies for which it was designed. The number of possible frequencies being infinite, I can construct an infinite number of motors among which there will not be two sensitive to identical waves. Do you still understand me?"

"It's harder," Barsac conceded, "but we can follow you all the same."

"I've finished, anyhow," said Camaret. "It is by their aid that we actuate numerous agricultural machines which draw their energy, some distance away, from one or other of the projections bristling from that tower. Similarly, that's the way we control the wasps. Each has four screws and contains four small-sized motors differing in syntonization, and we can actu-ate one or more of them as we wish. Finally, that is how I could destroy the whole town, if ever I should want to."

"You could destroy the town from here!" cried Barsac.

"Quite easily. Harry Killer asked me to make it impregnable

and I made it impregnable. Below every street, below all the houses, below the Palace and below the Factory itself, are powerful explosives, each with a detonator syntonized with waves known only to myself. To blow up the town, I need only send towards each of the mines waves with a frequency corresponding to its detonator."

Amédée Florence, who was feverishly taking notes, had a fleeting impulse to suggest that it would be as well to make use of this process to put an end to Harry Killer. But he remembered in time the scanty success obtained by his suggestion to use the aerial torpedoes for the same purpose, and prudently kept silent.

"And the large pylon on top of the tower?" asked Dr. Châtonnay.

"I'm coming to it, and I'll end with it," Camaret replied. "It's very strange that the so-called Hertzian waves act as though they were subject to the attraction of gravity: radiating from the point of emission, they incline slowly towards the earth, where they are finally lost.

"So if they are to be sent any distance they have to be generated at an appropriate height. For my purposes, that would be even more necessary, for my aim is to send them not to a great distance but to a great height, and that's more difficult still. But I have succeeded, thanks partly to a pylon a hundred yards high connected to the oscillator, partly to a reflector I invented, placed at the top of the pylon."

"Why do you want to send the waves upwards?" asked Amédée, who was rather out of his depth.

"To make rain. It is the basic principle of the invention I had in mind when I knew Harry Killer, and he helped me to accomplish it. By means of the pylon and the reflector I direct waves against the clouds, and I electrify to saturation point the raindrops they contain. When the difference of potential between a cloud and the earth or one of the adjacent clouds is great enough—and this does not take very long—a storm breaks, and the rain descends. The transformation of the desert into fertile country is quite enough to prove the efficiency of the process."

"But you've got to have the clouds," Dr. Châtonnay put in.

"Naturally—or at least a damp enough atmosphere. But clouds are bound to come some day or other. The problem is to break them here and not somewhere else. Now that the land is cultivated and the tree are beginning to grow, a series of regular rainfalls is tending to begin, and the clouds are getting more plentiful. As soon as one arrives this is all I have to do," explained Camaret, throwing over a switch, "and at once waves, emitted with a force of a thousand horse-power, bombard them with countless vibrations."

"Marvellous!" his hearers were enthusiastic.

"At this very moment, though you cannot in any way perceive it," he continued, more and more excited as he described his inventions, "waves are flowing from the summit of the pylon and losing themselves in the infinite. But I can imagine another future for them. I feel, I know, I'm certain, that they can be employed for a hundred different purposes. For example, it would be possible to communicate with the whole surface of the earth, by telegraph or telephone, without needing a wire to link the respective stations."

"Without a wire!" exclaimed his hearers.

"Without a wire. What would we need for that? Very little. I've only got to think out a suitable receiver. I'm working on it, I've almost got it, but I haven't quite got it yet."

"We're beginning to get out of our depth," Barsac protested.

"But nothing could be simpler," Camaret declared, his excitement growing. "Look, here's a Morse instrument, the type used in ordinary telegraphy, which I have placed experimentally in a special circuit. I've only to work these switches," which he was handling even as he spoke, "for the wave-producing current to be connected with the circuit. When the Morse key is raised, the Hertzian waves are not transmitted. When it is depressed, and only while it is depressed, the waves are emitted from the pylon.

"But now it is not towards the sky that the waves are to be projected but towards the hypothetical receiver. This is done by turning in the appropriate direction the reflector which concentrates them. If the direction is unknown, it will be enough simply to cut out the reflector, which I can do by means of this other switch. Now the waves emitted will spread into space in all directions around us, and I can telegraph and be certain that I shall reach the receiver—if there is one— wherever it may be. Unfortunately there isn't one."

"You said telegraph?" asked Jane Blazon. "What did you mean by that?"

"Just what one usually means. I have only to use the switch in the ordinary way, making use of the Morse alphabet, which all telegraphists understood. But it will help you if I give an example. If that hypothetical receiver existed, you would take the first opportunity of using it to get out of your present position, I imagine?"

"There's no question about that!" said Jane.

"Well, act as if it were there," Camaret suggested, sitting before the Morse apparatus. "Whom would you telegraph to in that case?"

"In a country where we don't know anyone," Jane said smilingly. "I might well ask who. . . . I only know Captain Marcenay," she added with a slight blush.

"Let's make it Captain Marcenay," agreed Camaret; as he spoke the Morse key was tapping out the longs and shorts of its alphabet. "Whereabouts is he?"

"I think he's at Timbuctoo just now," said Jane hesitatingly.

"Timbuctoo," Camaret repeated, still working the key. "Now what do you want to say to Captain Marcenay? Something of this sort, I suppose 'Jane Blazon. . . .'"

"Excuse me," Jane interrupted him, "Captain Marcenay only knows me under the name of Jane Mornas."

"That doesn't matter, as the message will never arrive, still let's make it Mornas. So I'm sending: 'Come to the rescue of Jane Mornas held prisoner at Blackland. . . .'"

Here Marcel Camaret interrupted himself :

"And, as Blackland seems to be unknown to the outer world, I shall explain its situation, so I'll add : 'latitude 15°.50 north, longitude. . . .' "

He jumped up from his seat.

"There !" he exclaimed, "Harry Killer has cut off the current."

Failing to realize the position, his guests crowded round him.

"As I told you," he explained, "the power reaches us from a hydro-electric station installed about six miles up-stream. Harry Killer has cut us off from that station, that's all."

"But then the machines will stop !" said Dr. Châtonnay.

"They've stopped already," Camaret replied.

"And the wasps ?"

"They've fallen to earth, there's no doubt about that."

"Then Harry Killer can use them," cried Jane Blazon.

"That's not so certain," the engineer replied. "Come up to the top, and you'll see he has not gained anything."

Quickly climbing to the higher floors, they entered the cycloscope. As before, they at once saw the outer face of the wall, together with the dyke around it; in its depths lay the motionless wasps.

On the Esplanade the Merry Fellows were shouting in triumph. Already they were returning to the attack. Some of them jumped into the dyke and laid their hands on the dead wasps, which had scared them so much while they were alive.

But they had scarcely touched them when they showed signs of disquiet. Recoiling in fright, they hastened to climb out of the dyke. A few of them were too weak to succeed, and one after another they fell unconscious.

"I would not give two sous for their lives," Marcel Camaret said coldly. "You may well believe that I foresaw what would happen and took my precautions accordingly. In cutting off the current from the station, Harry Killer has *ipso facto* opened a sluice through which containers of liquid carbon dioxide have emptied into the dyke, where it at once resumed the gaseous state. Being heavier than air, the gas remains in the dyke, and anyone in it must inevitably die of asphyxiation."

"Poor fellows!" exclaimed Jane Blazon.

"The worse for them," Camaret declared, "I can't do anything to help them. Regarding my machines, I've also taken precautions. Since this morning liquid air—I have an inexhaustible supply of it—has replaced the current from the generating station, and now that's the motive power of my electrical machines. That's already been done—and look, the machines are working. The wasps are again in flight."

The screws of the wasps had again begun their bewildering spin, and the machines had resumed their protective circling. Meanwhile the crowd of Merry Fellows, forsaking their comrades who lay in the dyke, had retired to the Palace.

Marcel Camaret turned towards his guests. He seemed nervous—even abnormally agitated—and the disquieting light which they had already noticed was once again marring the clearness of his gaze.

"We can sleep in peace, I fancy," he said, a little puffed up with naïve vanity.

CHAPTER VIII

A CALL INTO SPACE

VERY sadly Captain Marcenay left the Barsac Mission, and especially the lady whom he knew as Jane Mornas. He went off, however, without the slightest hesitation, and as far as Ségou-Sikoro he travelled, as commanded, by forced march. He was first and foremost a soldier, and it may be the greatness of the military profession to demand complete self-sacrifice and absolute obedience towards ends which may not be self-evident but which are always dominated by the ideal of patriotism.

Hasten as he might, however, it took nine days to cross the three hundred miles which separated him from Ségou-Sikoro, and it was not until the 22nd February, at a late hour of the evening, that he arrived. So it was only on the following morning that he could report to Colonel Sergines, the commandant, and show him Colonel Saint-Auban's order.

Colonel Sergines read the order three times with increasing surprise. He did not seem to understand it.

"What an unusual procedure!" he said at last. "To call for men at Sikasso to send them to Timbuctoo! It's unimaginable!"

"Then you weren't told we were coming, mon Colonel?" the Captain asked.

"Decidedly not."

"The lieutenant who brought me the order," Marcenay explained, "said that unrest had broken out at Timbuctoo, and that the Touareg Aouelimmeden were dangerously astir."

"It's the first I've heard of it," the colonel declared. "Yesterday, in fact, Captain Peyrolles . . . perhaps you know him?"

"Yes, mon Colonel. Two years ago we served in the same regiment."

"Well, he went through here, Peyrolles did, *en route* from

Timbuctoo to Dakar. He left only yesterday, and he never said a word about it."

All that Captain Marcenay could do was to make a gesture disavowing all responsibility.

"You're right, Captain," said Colonel Sergines. "It's not our place to argue. There is the order, and it will have to be obeyed. But the devil knows when you can set out, I must say."

It took some trouble, indeed, to get ready for that unforeseen expedition. More than eight days were taken up in finding stabling for the horses, who had been ordered to be left at Ségou-Sikoro and to collect enough food and transport for the journey. It was only on the 2nd of March that Captain Marcenay was able to embark and begin the descent of the Niger.

The journey, often held up by the low level of the river in the last months of the dry season, then took two full weeks. So it was not until the 17th March that the former escort of the Barsac Mission disembarked at Kabara, the port of Timbuctoo, about ten miles distant.

When Captain Marcenay reported to Colonel Allègre, the local commandant, that officer showed the same surprise as his colleague at Ségou-Sikoro. He declared that no trouble had been located in the region, that he had never asked for reinforcements, and that he could not explain why Colonel Saint-Auban had sent him without notice a hundred men for whom he had no need.

This seemed very strange, and Captain Marcenay was beginning to wonder if he had been taken in by a skilled forger. But why? What for? The answer was obvious. Inexplicable as the scheme might appear, the forgery could have no other purpose than to destroy the unprotected Barsac Mission. Logically forced to that conclusion, Captain Marcenay felt acute anguish when he thought of the grave responsibility which he would have incurred, and the dangers which threatened Mlle Mornas, whose memory dominated his spirit and heart.

These fears became even more acute when he could no more learn at Timbuctoo than at Ségou-Sikoro anything whatever about Lieutenant Lacour; nobody knew of him. What was more, nobody had ever heard of a corps of Soudanese Volunteers, although these terms had been used by Colonel Saint-Auban himself.

None the less, as the colonel's order, when examined minutely, had every appearance of authenticity, it had to be regarded as genuine until proof could be obtained to the contrary. Quarters were therefore assigned to Captain Marcenay and his men : and as soon as an opportunity occurred, the order of Colonel Saint-Auban would be sent to its author, who alone could say whether or not it was apocryphal.

But from Timbuctoo to Bammako was over six hundred miles, as much uphill as down. Much time would therefore elapse before a reply could be received from the colonel.

For Captain Marcenay, at a loose end, without definite duties, and the prey to continual disquiet, that time would have seemed very long. Happily, however, towards the end of March, relief came in the person of Captain Perrigny, one of his old comrades at St. Cyr with whom he had never ceased to be on terms of intimate friendship. The two friends were delighted to see one another, and from that moment time passed more quickly for Captain Marcenay.

Informed of his comrade's uneasiness, Perrigny reassured him. He regarded the idea of a spurious order, so well counterfeited that it deceived everyone, as nonsensical. He thought it more likely that Lieutenant Lacour, badly informed as to the true motives for the Colonel's decision, had described them inaccurately. As for the surprise of Colonel Allègre, that was easy to explain. In a region not yet fully organized, it was not at all to be wondered at that an order should have gone astray.

Captain Perrigny, who was to be stationed two years at Timbuctoo, had brought a quantity of luggage with him, and his friend helped him unpack. Strictly speaking, much of it consisted of laboratory instruments rather than baggage. If he had not worn uniform, Perrigny would certainly have been placed among the savants. Devoted to science, he kept himself acquainted with all its current problems, and especially with those relating to electricity. In their relationship, Perrigny represented study and Marcenay action. This difference in their leanings frequently gave rise to friendly disputes. They were accustomed to call each other an old library rat and a low swashbuckler, but they fully realized that Marcenay's love of action did not keep him from being a cultivated and well-informed man, any more than Perrigny's learning interfered with his being a brave and competent officer.

A few days after his friend arrived, Captain Marcenay found that he had just installed a new apparatus in a yard of the dwelling where he had placed his household goods.

"You've come just at the right moment," Perrigny exclaimed. "I'm going to show you something interesting."

"That?" asked Marcenay, pointing towards some apparatus comprising two electric batteries, some electro-magnets, and a small glass tube containing some metallic filings, and surmounted by a copper upright several yards high.

"Just that," Perrigny replied. "This trifle, just as you see it here, is a real example of witchcraft. It's simply a telegraphic receiving station, but—mark my words—of *wireless telegraphy*."

"They've been talking about that for several years," Marcenay replied with interest. "Has the problem been solved?"

"It certainly has!" exclaimed Perrigny. "Yes, two men have appeared on this terrestrial globe at the same instant of history. One, an Italian called Marconi, has found a method of radiating into space the waves known as Hertzian. . . . Do you happen to know what they are, you hectoring ruffian?"

"Yes I do," replied Marcenay, "when I was in France they were discussing Marconi. But the other inventor you mentioned?"

"He's a Frenchman, Doctor Branly. It was he who discovered the receiver, a tiny marvel of simple ingenuity."

"And this apparatus I'm looking at?"

"That's the receiver—you'll understand its principle in a twinkling. M. Branly noticed that, although iron filings are normally poor conductors of electricity, they become excellent conductors under the action of an Hertzian wave. Its effect is to make them attract one another and increase their cohesion. That conceded, you see this little tube?"

"I can see it."

"This is the coherer, or wave-detector, whichever you like. This tube, which is full of iron filings, is inserted in the circuit of an ordinary battery which I have the honour to show you. Being a poor conductor, the tube consequently interrupts the circuit, and no current passes. Understand?"

"Yes, but then?"

"If then a Hertzian wave should arrive, it is captured by this copper rod, which is called an antenna. The tube, which is connected up with it, becomes a conductor, the battery circuit is closed, and the current passes. Do you still understand, you wallower in blood?"

"Yes, you old barnacle of a scientist. Go on."

"And this is where the present speaker comes in. Thanks to a contrivance which I invented myself, combined with Branly's discovery, the current activates a Morse receiver through which a paper tape unrolls in the ordinary way. But at the same time this little hammer which you see here taps the coherer; the shock separates the filings and these as usual become non-conductors. The current no longer flows from the battery, and the Morse receiver stops printing.

"That only makes one single point on the paper tape, you tell me? Yes, but the same series of events continues, so long as the antenna keeps on receiving the waves. When these stop, nothing is printed on the tape until the next waves arrive. So at last this action gives us a series of points in unequal groups, representing the longs and shorts of the Morse alphabet. A telegraphist can read them as easily as ordinary writing."

"You, for example?"

"Me, for example."

"And why have you brought this instrument—out of the ordinary, I must say—into these barbaric parts?"

"It and its brother, the wave producer, in other words the transmitter, which I shall start setting up to-morrow. I've a passion for wireless telegraphy. I want to be the first to instal it in the Sahara. That's why I've brought these two sets of equipment. Things like these are still rare enough anywhere on earth, and there are none of them in Africa, I can tell you that. Just think of it! If we could get directly into touch with Bammako. . . . And perhaps with St. Louis!"

"With St. Louis! . . . That's a bit far!"

"Not at all," Perrigny protested. "Long-distance communication has already been carried out."

"Impossible!"

"Quite possible, you war-battered veteran. And I hope to do even better myself. I'm going to begin a series of experiments all along the Niger. . . ."

Captain Perrigny stopped abruptly. His widely-opened eyes, his gaping mouth, showed how greatly he was surprised. From the Branly apparatus came a faint crackling sound which his practised ear could recognize.

"What's up with you?" asked Marcenay in astonishment.

His friend had to make an effort to reply. His amazement seemed to strangle him. "It's going," he said at last, pointing to the apparatus.

"What! It's going," Captain Marcenay replied ironically. "You're dreaming, you future member of the Institute. Your apparatus is the only one in Africa, so it can't possibly be going as you put it so elegantly. It's out of order, that's all."

Captain Perrigny hastened to the receiver without replying.

"Out of order!" he protested, seized by violent excitement. "It's so little out of order that I can read on the tape: 'Capt . . . ain . . . Capt . . . ain . . . Mar . . . Captain Marcenay!' "

"My name!" his friend chaffed him. "I'm much afraid, old man, that you're not going to have *me* on, as they say."

"Your name!" declared Perrigny, speaking with so much emotion that his comrade was impressed.

The apparatus had stopped and now remained silent under the eyes of the two officers, who were still staring at it. Soon, however, the significant clicking could be heard once more.

"Look at it starting again!" exclaimed Perrigny, who was leaning over the tape. "Well! Now it's your address: 'Timbuctoo'."

"Timbuctoo!" Marcenay repeated mechanically. He too was trembling, gripped by a strange emotion.

The apparatus had stopped a second time. Then after a brief pause, the printed tape again began to unroll, only to stop once more a few moments later.

"Jane Blazon," Perrigny read aloud.

"Don't know her," Marcenay declared, giving, though he hardly knew why, a sigh of relief. "It's a trick somebody's playing on us."

"A trick?" Perrigny repeated thoughtfully. "Why, how could anyone—look, it's started again."

Leaning over the tape he read, spelling out the words as fast as they appeared:

"Come . . . to . . . the . . . res . . cue . . . of . . . Jane . . . Mor . . . nas."

"Jane Mornas!" exclaimed Captain Marcenay. Feeling that he was choking, he unhooked the collar of his tunic.

"Quiet!" Perrigny ordered. "Pri . . . son . . . er . . . at . . . Black . . . land . . ."

For the fourth time the clicking stopped. Perrigny stood upright and looked at his comrade, who had turned very pale. "What's wrong?" he asked affectionately.

"I'll explain later," Marcenay replied painfully. "But Blackland, what do you make of Blackland?"

Perrigny had no time to reply. The apparatus was working yet once again. He read:

"Lat . . . it . . . ude . . . Fif . . . teen . . . de . . . grees . . . fif . . . ty . . . min . . . utes . . . north . . . long . . . it . . . ude. . . ."

Leaning over the instrument which had suddenly fallen silent, the two officers waited in vain for some minutes. This time the stop was final, and the Morse receiver was dumb.

Captain Perrigny murmured very thoughtfully : "That's a strong cup of tea, as the saying is. Can there be another wireless amateur in this God-forsaken country? And someone who knows you, old man," he added.

Turning towards his friend, he was struck by the alteration in his face. "Is anything the matter?" he asked. "You look quite pale."

In a few quick words, Captain Marcenay told his comrade the reason for his distress. If his surprise had been great when he saw his own name appearing on the tape, it had become emotion, and a deep emotion, when Perrigny had pronounced that of Jane Mornas. He knew Jane Mornas, he loved Jane Mornas, and though no word had been said on the matter between them, it was his steadfast hope that one day she would become his wife.

He recalled the fears which had tormented him ever since he had so much reason to doubt the validity of Colonel St. Auban's orders. The mysterious message which had just arrived out of space had confirmed them only too well. Jane Mornas was in danger.

"And it was I whom she turned to for help !" he exclaimed, his distress not unmingled with a trace of joy.

"Well, that's easy enough," replied Perrigny. "You must give her the help she asks for."

"That goes without saying !" exclaimed Marcenay, excited by the prospect of action. "But how?"

"We shall have to look into that," Perrigny told him. "Let's first draw out the logical conclusions of the facts we know. I find them reassuring."

"You find them? . . ." Marcenay replied bitterly.

"Yes, I do. *Primo,* Mlle Mornas cannot be alone, for as you know she never had a wireless transmitter. Not to speak of the companions you left with her, she must have at least one protector, the one who owns that apparatus. And he's an expert, you can take my word for it."

On Marcenay's giving an approving nod, Perrigny continued :

"*Secundo,* Mlle Mornas is not exposed to immediate peril. She telegraphed you at Timbuctoo. That's where she thinks you are, so she must know that you're on the far side of the door, and will take some time to answer her call. Then since she telegraphed you in spite of that, she must think it wouldn't be in vain. So, if danger threatens her, it isn't imminent."

"What are you suggesting?" Marcenay asked nervously.

"That you set your mind at ease, with good hopes that the story will end happily . . . and go and find the colonel and ask him to organize an expedition to rescue M. le Député Barsac—and Mlle Mornas into the bargain."

The two captains at once went to Colonel Allègre, to whom they related the astonishing events they had just witnessed. They showed him the tape printed by the Morse receiver, which Perrigny translated into "clear."

"There's nothing about M. Barsac there," the colonel pointed out.

"No," replied Perrigny, "but as Mlle Mornas was with him. . . ."

"Who told you she hasn't left him?" the colonel objected. "I know the route of the Barsac Mission quite well, and I can guarantee that it didn't extend so high in latitude. The Mission was to pass through Ouaghadougou, which is well known to be on the twelfth degree, and to end at Saye, which is on the thirteenth. This mysterious message talks about fifteen degrees fifty—sixteen degrees one might say."

This comment aroused Marcenay's memory.

"You're right, mon Colonel," he agreed. "Mlle Mornas may indeed have left the Barsac Mission. I recollect that she meant to set off a hundred miles or so beyond Sikasso, to go north-wards alone, with the aim of reaching the Niger at Gao."

"That alters the look of things," the colonel replied seriously, "to free M. Barsac, a Deputy, an official delegate of France, an expedition would be reasonable, while for Mlle Mornas, a private individual. . . ."

"None the less," Marcenay interrupted with energy, "if the order I brought was false, as everything leads us to suppose, M. Barsac must be the victim of that rascal who took my place."

"Maybe . . . maybe," the colonel conceded doubtfully. "But to clear that matter up, we must wait for a reply from Bammako."

"But it's urgent," Marcenay cried distressfully. "We cannot let that poor child perish when she's appealed to me for help."

"It isn't a question of perishing," the colonel objected; he, at least, had retained his calm. "She only says that she's a prisoner, nothing more. . . . Besides, where would you go to rescue her? What's this Blackland she's talking about?"

"She's given us the latitude."

"Yes, but not the longitude. Well, you left Mlle Mornas beyond Sikasso. She hasn't gone back westwards, I suppose. The sixteenth degree first traverses the Macina, then crosses the Niger, and vanishes into a desert region which is absolutely unknown. Blackland couldn't possibly be in the Macina without our knowing about it, so we should have to look for it in the open desert."

"Well, mon Colonel? . . ." ventured Marcenay.

"Well, Captain, I don't see how I can possibly send a column in that direction. That would come to risking the lives of a hundred or two hundred men to rescue only one individual."

"Why two hundred men?" asked Marcenay, who felt his hopes vanishing. "Surely far fewer would be ample."

"I don't think so, Captain. You cannot be unaware of the rumours travelling all along the Niger. The blacks say that somewhere or other—nobody can tell exactly where—there is a native empire which hasn't the best of reputations. As the name Blackland is unknown, it isn't impossible that it should be that of the capital or one of the towns of the empire in question. The latitude you have been given renders this idea more feasible, for this is the only region where such a power could have been founded without all the world's knowing about it.

"Besides, doesn't the English sound of the word 'Blackland' strike you? . . . Sokoto, an English colony, is not so far from its supposed position. . . . That might create another difficulty, not one of the least prickly. . . . In short, granted such conditions, I feel that it would be imprudent to risk an adventure in a region completely unexplored, without using sufficient forces to meet every eventuality."

"Then, mon Colonel, you refuse?" Marcenay insisted.

"With regret, but I must refuse," replied Colonel Allègre.

Captain Marcenay insisted still further. He explained to his chief, as he had explained to his comrade, the ties which bound him to Mlle Mornas. It was in vain. It was equally in vain that he pointed out that he had brought with him a hundred men who could be spared because nobody had expected them. Colonel Allègre would not let himself be moved.

"I am distressed, profoundly distressed, Captain, but it is my duty to reply in the negative. Possibly your men may not be needed here, but they are men, and I haven't the right to jeopardize their existence so lightly. Besides, there is no urgency. Let us wait for another communication from Mlle Mornas. As she has telegraphed once, quite possibly she'll telegraph again."

"And if she doesn't," Marcenay protested despairingly, "what are we to deduce from the sudden interruption of her message?"

The colonel made a gesture indicating that this was infinitely regrettable, but that it could not modify his decision.

"Then I shall go alone," Marcenay declared firmly.

"Alone?" the colonel repeated.

"Yes, mon Colonel. I shall ask for leave of absence, which you cannot refuse. . . ."

"On the contrary, which I shall refuse," the colonel replied. "Do you think I shall let you throw yourself into an adventure from which you may never return?"

"In that case, mon Colonel, I must ask you to be good enough to accept my resignation."

"Your resignation!"

"Yes, mon Colonel," Marcenay replied calmly.

Colonel Allègre did not reply at once. He looked at his subordinate, and realized that the man was not in a normal state of mind.

"You realize, Captain," he replied in fatherly tones, "that your resignation would have to go through the official channels, and that I haven't the authority to accept it. In any event, it is something which needs to be reflected on. Let's leave it for to-night and come and see me to-morrow. We must have a chat."

Giving a formal salute, the two officers left him. Perrigny walked away with his comrade, trying as best he could to reassure him. But the unfortunate man did not even hear him.

When Captain Marcenay reached his quarters, he took leave of his friend and locked himself in. Alone at last, he threw himself on his bed, and his courage exhausted, unable to bear any more, he burst into sobs.

CHAPTER IX

DISASTER

THE interruption of the current from the hydro-electric station did not last long. Cut off on the 9th April, the current again began to flow on the following morning.

In point of fact, Harry Killer was the first victim of that manœuvre, which he had thought so very clever. If he no longer supplied to the Factory the energy it needed, in return this no longer rendered him the services he was used to.

The agricultural machines, robbed of the waves which gave them life, had suddenly stopped.

The electric pumps which raised water from the river to fill the two reservoirs had similarly ceased to function. One, in the Factory itself, supplied another above the barracks of the Black Guard. In two days this second reservoir, whence the water was distributed everywhere, had run dry, and Blackland was without water.

Then, after nightfall, there was no longer any electric light, and as there was no other means of illumination, the whole town was plunged into darkness. This enraged Harry Killer, the more because all this time he could see the Factory well lit and protected by the beams of its powerful searchlights.

Realizing at last that the dice were loaded against him, the despot resigned himself to restoring, from the morning of 10th April, the current which he had cut off the day before. At the same time he made a telephone call to Marcel Camaret, who happened to be in his office with those whom he had agreed to protect.

These heard the engineer reply, as previously, with the words "yes", "no", and "good", which are the small change of such conversation when half remains unknown to the bystanders. Again as before, he curtly interrupted the dialogue with a burst of laughter.

According to the summary he gave his guests, Harry Killer

119

and he had reached an agreement. It was decided that the former should resume the supply of current from the hydro-electric station, and that for its part the Factory should guarantee the general services of Blackland. This agreement, however, did not at all alter the rest of the situation, which did not cease to be extraordinary. The peace was limited to the terms agreed. For the rest, it was still to be war. Harry Killer especially persisted in demanding his prisoners, and Marcel Camaret in refusing to give them up.

At the end of the conversation, Harry Killer had asked the engineer to let him have the liquid air he needed for his heliplanes. Every time these returned from a journey their fuel-tanks were empty and were left at the Factoy to be re-filled. Harry Killer no longer possessed a drop of the liquid air, and this had put his forty flying-machines out of action.

On this point Marcel Camaret, equally anxious both to con-serve his supply of motive power and not to provide the enemy with weapons so powerful, had point-blank refused. There-upon the despot had flown into a rage, and had vowed to starve the factory out. It was then that the engineer had replaced the receiver, laughing at a threat which seemed as vain as its predecessors.

His hearers, however, took it very seriously indeed. If the Factory really seemed impregnable, thanks to the defences which Camaret had designed, it seemed to be less well provided with aggressive weapons, and moreover he would not at any price use those he possessed. Under such conditions, the situation could last indefinitely, and at last a day would come when hunger would force the Factory to surrender.

When Barsac consulted him about it, Camaret shrugged his shoulders. "We've got enough provisions for some time," he assured him.

"For how long?" Barsac asked.

Camaret made an evasive gesture. "I don't know exactly. Fifteen days, maybe three weeks. That's unimportant, how-ever, because in forty-eight hours we shall have completed a heliplane which is now under construction. For the moment I invite you to take part in its trial, which we shall carry out by night, so that the Palace will not see it. It will take place the day after to-morrow, the 12th April, at four in the morning."

This was good news, which the prisoners had not at all expected. To have that heliplane would certainly much improve their situation. But would it bring rescue?

"There are more than a hundred people in the Factory," Barsac pointed out. "However powerful it may be, your heliplane cannot carry them all."

"It will only take ten people," Camaret replied, "not counting the pilot. That's not too bad."

"Excellent!" Barsac agreed, "and yet it won't be enough to get you out of this business."

"Not at all," replied Camaret. "From Saye it is about two hundred miles as the crow flies, and about four hundred and fifty from Timbuctoo, which might be better. As we could only travel by night, to escape the aerial torpedoes, the heliplane can make three voyages in forty-eight hours to Saye or two to Timbuctoo. The five hundred people or so whom I estimate to be the population of the factory, women and children included, could be evacuated in five days by the first route or less than eight by the second."

The announcement of this plan, which seemed quite feasible, weakened the fears aroused by Harry Killer's threats. The chance to put it into operation was impatiently awaited.

To the besieged garrison the two days they had to wait seemed interminable. They spent the time as best they could, usually in walking about the garden, sheltered by the wall which hid them from the Palace. M. Poncin, in particular, lingered there from morning till night. Continually bending over the various plants it contained, he made measurements with a lens, and recorded weights very accurately by means of a small precision-balance.

"What the devil are you at?" asked Florence, when he surprised him engaged in this occupation.

"It's my work, Monsieur Florence," M. Poncin replied, not without an air of self-importance.

"Statistics?" asked Florence in amazement.

"Nothing else. I am simply working out the number of inhabitants which the Niger Bend would support."

"Aha, it's always the Bend," said Amédée Florence, who did not appear to take the work of his comrade very seriously. "It seems to me, however, that just here we're no longer in that famous Bend."

"There's no reason why we shan't work by analogy," M. Poncin proclaimed in academic tones.

"Flatterers who share in a splendid orgy!" remarked a voice behind them.

By this quotation from the *Châtiments*,[1] brought in for the sake of the rhyme, Amédée Florence recognized Dr. Châtonnay.

"What are you doing there?" asked the good-hearted fellow, having finished his quotation.

"M. Poncin is explaining statistical technique," Florence replied in serious tone. "Please go on, M. Poncin."

"It's quite simple. Here's some spinach, taking up about four square inches. A little further on you can see a cauliflower; it takes up sixteen square inches. I've measured a hundred plants selected at random, and I've taken the average of the areas they occupy. I've similarly measured their daily growth. This lettuce, for example, has increased by exactly sixty one point seven to eighty grains since yesterday. In short, I have ascertained math-em-at-ic-al-ly, that the daily growth is about point three three nine of a grain to every nine-sixty-fourths of a square inch."

"That's very strange," Dr. Châtonnay declared without batting an eyelid.

"Yes, isn't it? These scientific enquiries are always quite interesting," said M. Poncin, throwing out his chest. And he

[1] A poetic satire by Victor Hugo, denouncing the leading figures of the Second Empire—I.O.E.

proceeded to work out from the area of the Niger Bend the weight of the crops it could produce—"12,012,000 tons a day or a yearly total of over a thousand million ton."

"I cannot deny that these figures are fun," hummed the doctor, parodying a line from Corneille whose rhythm had just come into his head.

"Knowing the amount of food needed to support the life of one man, it is easy to deduce the population which the Niger Bend can support," M. Poncin ended calmly. "Such are the services which science can render, and so our imprisonment will not be completely wasted."

"Thanks to you, Monsieur Poncin," Amédée Florence and the doctor declared with one voice. And they left the statistician to his researches.

Hour by hour passed the 10th and then the 11th.

One incident, though without importance, broke the monotony of the second day. About five in the afternoon Camaret was told that the pump which raised water from the river was no longer working.

The engineer confirmed the report. The pump was running wild, as though it were working in the void and meeting with no resistance. He ordered the piston to be taken out, for its flanges seemed to have been damaged so that they did not fit the bore of the cylinder. This was only a matter of a trifling repair which could be completed in less than forty-eight hours.

By dawn of the next day this nerve-racking wait was at last over. As might be supposed, in spite of the early hour fixed by Marcel Camaret, nobody was missing at the *rendez-vous*. He for his part had kept his promise. When they reached the garden, where the trials were to be made, the workmen who had built the heliplane had already brought it out.

The engineer climbed on to the platform and tuned up the motor. Several minutes elapsed, too slowly to please the onlookers, who feared there might be some mistake. They were soon reassured. The apparatus suddenly rose easily; then, unfurling its wings, it glided through the air and returned to alight on the spot whence it had set out. Marcel Camaret, now taking ten men with him, soared aloft with it again, and three times flew around the garden. The experiment was over.

"To-night, at nine, the first flight," he announced as he left the platform.

At that all was forgotten—the siege, the imprisonment, the fortnight of anxiety and boredom. In a few hours the nightmare would be over. They would be free. They congratulated one another and exchanged good wishes, while the mechanics moved the heliplane back under cover until it should emerge, next evening, to take flight for Timbuctoo.

As the evacuation of the Factory would need several days, the usual work must not be interrupted. In particular the taking-down of the pump was completed that day. When this was done, the conclusion was reached that it was not damaged. The cause of the trouble would have to be sought elsewhere, and for the moment the pump only needed to be re-installed, a job that was done at once.

At half past eight in the evening, the darkness being complete, Marcel Camaret at last gave the signal to depart. Long before that Harry Killer's eight escaped prisoners and two of the wives of the workmen, who were to form the first convoy, were waiting in the garden, whence, under the control of an experienced pilot, the heliplane was to take flight. On the order of their chief, a dozen of the technicians went towards the shelter. They opened the door. . . .

That was the exact moment of the catastrophe.

At the very instant when the door opened, there came the sudden roar of a tremendous explosion. The shelter collapsed like a house built of playing-cards, leaving nothing but a pile of rubble.

After a moment's understandable amazement, the onlookers rushed to the help of the workmen. Fortunately, except for one slightly wounded, they had escaped scot-free, the explosion having taken place before they went into the shelter.

But although there were no deaths to lament, it was none the less a great misfortune, an irreparable disaster, which the garrison had suffered. The heliplane was destroyed, blown almost piece-meal. There remained nothing, but nothing but useless fragments.

"Rigaud," said Camaret, with the calm which never left him in the gravest circumstances, "start clearing up the site. We must learn the cause of the explosion."

They attacked the heap of ruins at the very spot where the heliplane had stood. The arms were many, and the work progressed rapidly. By about eleven, that part of the shelter flooring was laid bare, and beneath it was found a deep pit.

"Dynamite," Camaret said coldly. "It did not come here by itself, I suppose."

Bloodstains on the rubble having shown that the explosion had claimed its victims, work was continued with the same ardour. Soon, indeed, grim discoveries were made. A little before midnight, they included the torn-off arm of a negro. Then came a hand violently ripped off, and last was found the head belonging to that mutilated body.

Amédée Florence, who, like a good reporter, had watched the work attentively, recognized that dismal trophy at once :

"Tchoumouki !" he cried unhesitatingly.

He explained to Camaret who the fellow was, a traitor from the service of Miss Blazon into that of Harry Killer. That, in fact, explained everything. Tchoumouki was at once the cause and the victim of the explosion. It only remained to be learned how he had found his way into the factory.

Anyhow, as he had done so, others might have followed by the same route. It was now a matter of foiling the plans of the enemy by striking them with a salutary terror.

For this purpose, Camaret ordered the mangled remains of Tchoumouki to be thrown over the wall on to the Esplanade, where Harry Killer's followers could not fail to find them. They would thus learn, without any shadow of doubt, that to get into the Factory was not devoid of danger.

Meanwhile the clearing-up continued. The workmen passed the debris from hand to hand, the rubbish piled up in the garden, and the rest of the surface of the shelter was uncovered bit by bit.

"Here's another of them!" one of the workmen cried suddenly.

Marcel Camaret went across. A human foot was indeed appearing between the fragments. A few minutes later the whole body was uncovered. It was a white man in the prime of life, his shoulder horribly mangled by the fall of the roofing.

Doctor Châtonnay bent over him. "He's still alive!" he announced.

The man was freed of the rubbish and brought to Camaret, while the doctor applied first-aid. Next day they would interrogate him if he had strength to speak.

"And if he's willing to," remarked Amédée Florence.

"I'll undertake to see he's willing," said Marcel Camaret between his clenched teeth.

The clearing-up could now be regarded as complete. At least it had got so far they could be certain there was nobody else to be found in the ruins. So Marcel Camaret called off the work, and sent the workmen to get a well-earned rest.

Following their example, the engineer and his guests left the scene of the disaster and made off through the garden to their respective quarters.

But after a few paces Amédée Florence paused and asked Camaret: "What are we going to do, Sir, now we haven't got a heliplane?"

"We shall make another," Camaret replied.

"You've got the material?" asked Barsac.

"To be sure."

"How long will it take."

"Two months."

"Hum!" was Florence's only reply; and without pressing the matter further he walked thoughtfully away.

Two months! . . . And they only had food for a fortnight!

The reporter was already trying to think of a way out of this predicament.

CHAPTER X

AMÉDÉE FLORENCE HAS AN IDEA

How different from that of the previous day was the morning of the 13th April! Yesterday, sure of reaching the end of
their trials, the captives had exulted. To-day, all hope fled,
they were discouraged and sad.

Few of them had been able to sleep during the rest of the
night. Most of them had spent it going over the situation in
all its aspects, and found no means of overcoming its difficulties.

Marcel Camaret himself was at a loss. Short of building
another heliplane, he could imagine no way out of the present
difficulty. But to set his hopes on an apparatus which would
take two long months to build, when there was only food
enough for a fortnight, was not even to deceive himself.

Enquiry showed that this chance of escape was even less
feasible than they had supposed. A careful inventory of the
reserves and a careful examination of the horticultural products now growing to maturity made it clear indeed that
they had not even fifteen days' supplies but merely nine or
ten days! Not only before two months, but before the end
of the present month of April, they were bound to suffer
hunger.

To postpone as long as possible that inevitable calamity,
they decided to put themselves on rations at once. If they
could not flatter themselves that they might escape that fate,
they could at least prolong the agony of their siege.

The morning of the 13th was devoted to this inventory and
to work on the heliplane which Marcel Camaret was determined to construct although to all appearance there was no
hope of its rescuing them. So it was only during the afternoon that they could attend to the prisoner.

After a lunch, which for the first time was too scanty,
Camaret, accompanied by the guests whose sudden irruption

into his life threatened to cost him so dear, went up to the injured man, whom Doctor Châtonnay said was in condition to stand the enquiry.

"Who are you?" Camaret asked him. In asking this question, which seemed devoid of interest, he was conforming to a plan very carefully thought out.

The victim not having replied, Camaret repeated his question with no more success.

"I ought to warn you," the engineer said gently, "that I'm going to make you talk."

That threat did not make the man open his mouth, and his lips outlined an ironical smile. Make him talk? He plainly thought this incredible. And, indeed, to judge by his appearance, they were in the presence of an individual of no common energy.

Camaret shrugged his shoulders. Then, without insisting, he placed on the thumbs and under the feet of the recalcitrant four little metallic plates, and connected them up to some terminals. This done, he suddenly threw over a switch.

The man at once twisted in frightful convulsions. The veins on his neck were swollen as though about to burst, and his empurpled face displayed intolerable suffering.

The trial did not last long. After a few seconds, Camaret switched off the current. "Will you talk?" he asked.

Then, as the man remained quiet: "Very good!" he said. "Let's start again."

As again he completed the circuit the same results followed even more violently than before. The victim's face was covered with sweat, his eyeballs rolled upwards and his chest panted like the bellows of a forge.

"Will you talk?" Camaret asked, again cutting off the current.

"Yes . . . yes!" the man babbled; he was at the end of his strength.

"Excellent!" exclaimed Camaret. "What's your name?"

"Fergus David," came the answer.

E

"That's not a name," Camaret objected. "Those are two forenames."

"That's what they call me in Blackland. Nobody there knows my real name."

"That doesn't matter. What is it?"

"Daniel Frasne."

"Nationality?"

"English."

Daniel Frasne—for that really was his name—as determined to answer as briefly as he had previously been to keep silence, replied one by one to the questions put to him.

"Now, my lad," Camaret began. "I want some information. If you refuse, we'll carry on with the little game you've been playing. Do you feel inclined to let me have it?"

"Yes," the injured man replied.

"First of all, what's your position in Blackland? What part do you play there?"

"Counsellor."

"Counsellor?" repeated Camaret interrogatively.

Frasne seemed surprised that the engineer did not know the word. But he explained : "That's what they call those who share in Harry Killer's government."

"Then, if I understand you right, you share in the government of Blackland."

"Yes."

Marcel Camaret seemed quite satisfied with that reply. He continued : "Have you been here long."

"Since it started.

"You knew Harry Killer before that?"

"Yes."

"Where were you when you knew him."

"With Blazon's column."

On hearing these words, Jane trembled. Fate had provided her with another witness.

But Camaret repeated : "With Blazon's column : how is it I don't recognize you?"

"I suppose I must have altered," Frasne replied philosophically. "All the same I was with you, Monsieur Camaret."

Unable to wait any longer, Jane Blazon intervened. "Excuse me, Monsieur Camaret," she said, "but would you allow me to say a few words to this man?"

Camaret having agreed, she asked : "As you were with Blazon's column, you must have seen Harry Killer when he arrived?"

"Yes."

"Why did Captain Blazon give him so hearty a welcome?"

"I don't know anything about that."

"Would it be correct," Jane continued, "to say that from the day when Harry Killer joined the column, he became its real commander?"

"Quite correct," replied Frasne, showing some astonishment at being questioned about what had happened so long ago.

"So it was only by Harry Killer's orders that the Blazon column devoted itself to the acts of pillage which led to its being destroyed?"

"Yes," Frasne agreed.

"Captain Blazon had nothing to do with it?"

"No."

"You heard that, gentlemen?" asked Jane, turning towards her companions. Then, "Why was it," she enquired, "that Captain Blazon gave up his authority to Harry Killer?"

"How would you expect me to know that," Frasne answered impatiently.

He seemed sincere, and Jane thought it useless to insist. "At any rate, do you know how Captain Blazon died?" she asked, turning to another subject.

"Oh . . . in the fighting," Frasne replied, as if that went without saying. "Plenty of others fell at the same time."

Jane sighed. It was not in this way that she was going to clarify the many points which remained obscure.

"Thank you, sir," she said to Camaret. "I've finished."

The engineer at once recommenced his enquiries at the point where they had been interrupted.

"In the first place, how did they get hold of the negroes who built the town?" he asked.

Frasne opened his eyes widely. How could anyone ask so stupid a question? Good heavens, was this the sort of thing he'd just been tortured for?

"Obviously!" he said, "from the villages. You don't need much sense to know that!"

"Yes, but how?"

Frasne shrugged his uninjured shoulder. "That trick!" he said. "As if you didn't know! We simply took them."

"Ah!" . . . exclaimed Camaret, holding his head down with a dejected air.

"At the beginning, you needed machines. Where did they come from?"

"Not from the moon, to be sure!" sniggered Frasne.

"You got them from Europe?"

"Conceivably!"

"How did they get here?"

"They certainly didn't fly here. . . . Look, Monsieur Camaret, these are funny questions! How would you expect them to get here? They came in boats, that goes without saying."

"Where were they disembarked?" Camaret went on quietly.

"At Kotonou."

"But it's some distance from Kotonou to Blackland. How were they conveyed here?"

"Camels, horses, negroes," Frasne replied laconically; his patience seemed to be running out.

"During that long journey, many of the negroes died, I suppose?"

"More than the ones who were born!" grunted Frasne. "It wouldn't have amused me to count them."

Camaret went on to another subject: "These machines, they had to be paid for?"

"Hell!" exclaimed Frasne, who found these questions more and more nonsensical.

"Then there's money in Blackland."

"Certainly it isn't that we're short of!"

"Where did it come from?"

This time Frasne quite lost patience. "When are you going to leave off playing about with me, Monsieur Camaret?" he demanded in unfeigned anger, "asking me a heap of things you know better than I do? You didn't make those heliplanes just for fun. You know well enough that every now and again they took Harry Killer and his mates as far as the Bissago Islands, and then a steamer took them and brought them back after a little tour in Europe, in England mostly. It isn't you whom I've got to tell that in Europe there are banks, old misers and so forth, a whole lot of people whom it's worth while visiting . . . without an invitation. When the visit was over, they came back, and nobody saw them and nobody knew who they were."

"Did these journeys happen often?" Camaret asked, his face red with shame.

Frasne made a gesture of resignation. "Oh well, if this amuses you! . . ." he murmured. "It all depends—three or four times a year."

"And when was the last journey made?"

"The last?" replied Frasne, rummaging conscientiously among his memories. "Wait! . . . About four months ago, or four an a half."

"And whom did they visit that time?"

"I don't know very well," Frasne replied. "I wasn't in that · one. A bank, I think. But what I do know is that we'd never had such luck before."

Marcel Camaret was silent for a moment. He had turned quite pale and looked ten years older. "One last word, Frasne," he said. "How many negroes have you got working in the country?"

"About four thousand. Perhaps more."

"And women?"

"About fifteen hundred."

"And I suppose you got them the same as the others?"

"No," replied Frasne in quite natural tones. "Now there are the heliplanes to pick them up with."

"Ah! . . ." sighed Camaret. After another pause, he continued : "How did you get into here?"

Before replying Frasne hesitated for the first time. Here was a serious question at last! He was just as much annoyed at having to answer this as he had been ready to reply hitherto. Nevertheless, he had to. "Through the reservoir," he replied with a very ill grace.

"Through the reservoir?" Camaret asked in surprise.

"Yes. The day before yesterday the water-gates on the river were closed so that you couldn't pump up the water, and the reservoir at the Palace was emptied. This emptied the one at the Factory, which leads to the Palace by a conduit below the Esplanade. Tchoumouki and I came through that conduit."

A few hours before the engineer had learned, without paying it much attention, that the pump had been re-installed and was working perfectly. He now understood why Harry Killer, swayed by the frightful death of Tchoumouki, which he attributed to the defenders of the Factory, had re-opened the water-gate so that the water was flowing in as usual.

"That's well. I thank you," said Camaret. Having concentrated on the points that interested him, he went away without asking any more questions.

So the 13th dragged on, and on the 14th there was no fresh incident. The siege remained rigorous. On the quay upstream and on the Esplanade, the Merry Fellows were posted, and as their view extended everywhere around the encircling road and covered all the approaches to the Factory, nobody was able to leave it. There was no reason why the position should change until the day came when hunger would force the garrison to surrender.

That was the undeniable thought with which Amédée Florence was continually preoccupied. Since the heliplane had been destroyed, he had been looking for some way of getting out of this business, and he was angry at not being able to find one. At last, on the evening of the 14th, he had an idea. As that idea, looked at from all angles, seemed promising, next morning he had a long consultation with Tongané; then he asked his friends to come with him to Camaret, to whom he had something urgent to say.

Since Frasne had been questioned, nobody had seen the engineer, who had at once gone into his own quarters, where he still remained. There, alone, he was sadly working out the consequences of the facts revealed to him, and was hanging dizzily over the gulf which they implied.

He realized the entire truth. He knew that Blackland had been founded and maintained by violence, by robbery and murder. He knew that Europe and Africa had been, each in its own way, the scene of the exploits of Harry Killer and his followers. He could not shut his eyes to the origin of the gold so abundant in the town and thanks to which his work had been achieved. The atrocities committed by Blazon's column, the assassination of its leader, the continual slaughter of the hapless negroes, kidnapped from the villages, robberies, assassinations in Africa and Europe, and, to crown all, that abominable attack on the peaceful Barsac Mission—he understood them all.

In these innumerable crimes he felt himself implicated. In spite of his innocence, was it not indeed he who had furnished the means by which they were carried out? In realizing what his life had been over the last ten years, he was assailed by a very real terror, and his reason, already unstable, was yielding to the shock. Little by little he had come to detest this town of Blackland, which was none the less his own work, the flesh of his flesh, this pyramid of marvels which he himself had raised to his own glory. And indeed, could the atrocities of which its people were guilty remain unpunished? Was it not accursed, the very town which had been the scene of so much crime?

Amédée Florence and his companions found Camaret absorbed in his unhappy thoughts. Half stretched out in an armchair, motionless, his eyes dull, he seemed overcome and void of strength. In the two days during which nobody had seen him, he might not have taken any food.

Such a person was useless to Florence, who wanted to deal with the skilled inventor of the past. By his orders, Tongané was sent to look for some food. Camaret obediently ate it, but did not show the appetite which his long fast would have justified. After the meal, however, a little blood returned to his colourless face.

"The reason I've assembled all of you here," explained Florence, "is that I've hit on an idea for getting out of a situation from which there seems no escape. By dint of pondering over it, I have come to see quite clearly that we can secure a large number of allies that we've got so to speak close at hand."

"What allies?" Barsac and Dr. Châtonnay asked at once.

"The negroes in the slave quarter," replied Florence. "There must be at least four thousand of them, not counting the women, who ought to be as good as two men when they're set free. There's a force, it seems to me, which is not to be despised."

"That's clear," Barsac agreed, "but these negroes have no weapons, and probably they don't even know that we exist."

"That's the reason," said Florence, "why we must get into touch with them and arm them."

"That's easy to say!" exclaimed Barsac.

"And may be easy to do," Florence replied.

"Indeed?" asked Barsac. "Without mentioning the weapons, who's going to get in touch with these negroes?"

"A negro like themselves : Tongané."

"How will he get to them? You know well enough that the

Factory is surrounded. If he shows himself he'll be welcomed by a hail of bullets."

"So he mustn't go out of the door," explained Florence. "Besides that wouldn't help us, because just opposite to the Factory there's the White quarter. And it's the Black quarter he's got to reach. So the only thing to do is what he's done already—to reach the countryside during the night, lose himself in the crowd of negroes, and enter the town along with them."

"Then he'll have to go over the circular road and the wall?" Barsac objected.

"Or below them," replied Florence, turning towards Marcel Camaret.

But he, wrapped in thought, had remained outside the discussion, and seemed not even to have heard it.

"Monsieur Camaret," Florence asked him, "would it be possible to run a tunnel beneath the walls of the Factory and the town, a tunnel which would cross below the circular road and emerge in the open country?"

"Doubtless," agreed Camaret, lifting his head.

"How long would the work take?"

Camaret pondered for a moment. "In the ordinary way, we should have to dig the tunnel, and that would take a long time," he said. "But it could be shortened greatly by means of a machine I have just thought of, which would give excellent results in a sandy soil. To design that machine, to build it, and to drive the tunnel, a fortnight would be needed, and that would be quite enough."

"So you could get it finished by the end of the month?"

"Certainly," Camaret assured him.

As soon as anyone gave him a problem to solve he was again in his element. His mind was swinging into action, and he was visibly growing younger.

"A second point, Monsieur Camaret," Florence continued. "Will this tunnel need the help of all your staff?"

"It will need a good many," replied Camaret.

"Those who aren't needed for the work—could they manage to construct three or four thousand weapons in the same time?"

"What weapons? Not firearms, anyhow."

"Pikes, knives, axes, bludgeons, any sort of contrivances for stabbing, cutting or clubbing that you like."

"In that case, yes," agreed Camaret.

"And these weapons—could you manage to get them in due time to the slaves' quarter without Harry Killer's people seeing or hearing them?"

"That's more difficult," Camaret said quietly. He was silent for a few moments, then replied in his gentle voice. "Yes, I can manage that, provided the night is dark."

Amédée Florence gave a sigh of relief. "Then we're saved," he cried. "You understand, Monsieur Camaret, Tongané will go out through the tunnel, wait in the open until the black workers arrive and melt into them, and that evening he'll return with them. In the night he'll organize the revolt. All those people are wretchedly unhappy, and will ask only to throw off the yoke as soon as they've got weapons. As soon as you supply them, they won't hesitate. You must get to work at once, Monsieur Camaret."

"I'm at it already," was the engineer's only reply. Indeed, he had already settled down before his drawing-board.

The garrison went off much excited by the pleasant vista which Amédée Florence had revealed to their eyes. Yes, indeed, his idea was good, and it would have been absurd not to secure the help of these thousands of natural allies imprisoned on the far shore of the river. As for getting in touch with them, after the assurances of Camaret nobody doubted that this was possible. He had already given evidence on that point.

From the following day the construction of the heliplane was abandoned, and all the workmen were occupied, some in forging and sharpening pointed or edged weapons, others in constructing the new machine which Camaret had thought of, others again in hollowing out a treetrunk for some purpose which nobody understood, while the remainder were digging, out of sight of the Palace, a large well which deepened rapidly.

By the 21st April, the well had reached a depth of thirty feet. Camaret thought that enough, and began to drive a horizontal gallery. For this purpose he had devised a steel cone fifteen feet long and about four feet wide; its surface consisted of alternate ridges and grooves, arranged like a giant screw. An electric motor turned this apparatus, which, driving its point into the friable soil, literaly screwed itself forward; meanwhile the sand flowed through specially-made openings into the cone, when it was removed through the well.

When this gigantic screw was completely buried in the soil and at the same time supporting it, it was followed by a cylinder of the same size, driven after it by powerful screw-jacks. When the tunnel was complete, it would thus consist of a metallic tube about a hundred and fifty feet long.

When this was done, the perforated cone would be rotated so that a larger opening, hitherto closed, would be turned uppermost. Through this another smaller cone would be passed and screwed upwards until it reached the surface.

While these varied works were being carried out Camaret was hardly ever seen. He appeared, looking sombre and distraught, only when his presence was needed to solve any difficulty. This done, he again shut himself up in his own quarters, where in solitude he ate the meals which his servant Jacko prepared for him.

The tunnel was none the less completed in accordance with his plans.

By dawn on the 30th of April, the hundred and fifty feet of horizontal tubing were ready. At once began the installation of the smaller cone to bore the vertical exit, for this task had to be completed before daybreak.

It was time. From the 27th—three days before—food had begun to run short, and the rations, already inadequate, were cut down to next to nothing.

Good temper, or rather calmness in the face of life's difficulties, consorts ill with famished stomachs. Consequently the morale of the Factory staff began to deteriorate. Though they kept on working furiously, for their lives depended on it, their faces became more gloomy, and they exchanged angry words. They had plainly lost, to some extent at any rate, their blind confidence in their chief, to whom they had formerly attributed almost a supernatural power. For in spite of all his genius this magician had shown himself unable to keep them from dying of hunger, and his prestige had consequently suffered.

Moreover a legend had gradually sprung up, its origin being a few words regarding Jane Blazon spoken by Camaret in his introductory speech before hostilities had been opened against the Palace. At first Harry Killer's liking for her had been regarded as not very important, as merely one of the proofs of his despotic spirit which took its place among the rest.

But as the situation grew worse, as the sufferings increased, and especially as hunger clouded the mind, there was a growing tendency to regard Harry Killer's whim as being of first importance—although by now he himself might have forgotten about it. This idea, once it had got into the workmen's heads, could not be got rid of, and, like the well-known phenomenon of crystallization, it had absorbed all the others.

By now it had become an accepted fact. It was no longer a matter for discussion among the workers that if they were suffering, if they were undergoing hardships, if they were enduring a siege and were starving, it was solely because of the charms of Miss Blazon. If she would give herself up, peace would at once be restored. To go on to declare that the sacrifice was out of all proportion to its object, and that it was preposterous to condemn a hundred and fifty people to save one solitary individual, was only a step, and that was quickly taken.

Jane could not be unaware of this development in the

thoughts of the workmen. From the few words which reached her ears, the malevolent glances which she surprised when she crossed one or other of the workshops, she had inferred their dislike and realized that they regarded her as responsible for the risks they were running.

Although she was far from according to herself the importance implied in this opinion, she could not but be influenced by its unanimity. So, little by little, she came to feel that if she were to surrender to Harry Killer, that sacrifice would certainly have the effect of freeing the rest of the garrison.

Needless to say, it would be horrible to live with someone whom she vehemently suspected of being her brother's murderer. But apart from the fact that this accusation was not yet fully justified, if the effort went beyond her courage she could always seek refuge in death. Moreover, however dreadful it might be, this was undoubtedly her duty.

Gradually she became so fully convinced of this belief that she could no longer keep from disclosing it to her friends. She accused herself of cowardice, and talked of giving herself up to Harry Killer, on condition that this would assure the salvation of the others. On hearing her, poor St. Bérain cried as though his heart were broken.

"You're trying to dishonour us all, Mademoiselle," Amédée Florence declared indignantly, "and to dishonour us fruitlessly into the bargain! Harry Killer feels so certain of being able to get you one of these days that he will not pay the slightest price for his gratification. Besides, you can be certain he would never keep his promises even if he made them."

Barsac, Dr. Châtonnay, and even M. Poncin supported him, and Jane had to renounce a project as generous as it was absurd.

Now that the tunnel was finished, moreover, there was no longer any need for such a proposal. In a few hours Tongané was to escape, and on the following day he would no doubt give the signal for the revolt and the freeing of the garrison.

During the afternoon of the 30th, the smaller cone was put

in position, and at sunset it began to excavate the vertical well. Nothing delayed this part of the work. Before midnight the tube opened into the air, and the faithful Tongané vanished into the darkness.

The vertical tube was then withdrawn, and the sand, collapsing after it, completely filled the hole which it had left. On the surface of the ground there might remain a small funnel-shaped opening more or less deep, but in the absence of any other indication the besiegers could never imagine any relationship between this and the Factory, a hundred and fifty yards away.

If the plan of Blackland town had been accurate enough, it was clear that the upstream part of the Factory faced a corner of the wall between the White Quarter and from that of the slaves.

It was from that corner that when Tongané found the situation favourable, he was to give the signal to send on the weapons. It was therefore towards this point that, from the evening of the first of May, attention of the garrison was concentrated; they were grouped together on a scaffolding erected by Camaret above the workmen's houses nearest to the Red River.

As one might have expected, however, the first attempts were vain. Even if Tongané had succeeded in his enterprise, he could scarcely have arrived in the Black quarter. He needed time to explain matters and to organize the revolt.

On the next day, however, no signal could be seen, and the garrison began to get uneasy. They reassured themselves, however, by saying that that night the full moon was too brilliant for them to send on the weapons which were piled up in readiness upon the scaffolding.

Nevertheless, on the 3rd of May, the anxiety of the garrison became more intense, for that evening the dense clouds made the night dark in spite of the moon. Tongané's failure to act was especially serious because on that day the last fragments of food were consumed. Before two more days, or three at the most, they must either succeed, or surrender, or resign themselves to dying of hunger.

To the garrison it seemed that the 4th of May would never end, and they awaited the darkness with feverish impatience. But again that evening no signal appeared on the wall of the Blacks' quarters.

The 5th of May began under the most unhappy auspices. They had been fasting for two days, and their stomachs were crying out with hunger. The workshops were deserted. The workmen, their wives, and their children, wandered with furious looks about the Factory. Before another forty-eight hours, if nothing happened, they would have to give themselves up, bound hand and foot, to their conqueror.

Groups assembled and exchanged bitter words. They did not hesitate to accuse Tongané of having forgotten those whom he had promised to deliver. Indeed, they declared the negro would be very stupid if he worried about them!

Passing near one of these groups, Jane Blazon heard her name spoken. Surrounded by several of their comrades, a workman and a woman were arguing with as much violence as their weakness permitted, so violently indeed that Jane could stop and listen to them without being noticed.

"They can say what they like," the man shouted, careless of whether he was overheard or otherwise, "but all the same it's too much of a good thing to have to put up with all this for the sake of that little madam. If she belonged to me! . . ."

"Aren't you ashamed to talk like that?" asked the woman.

"Ashamed! . . . You're joking, mother! . . . I've got a kid in the family, I have, and he's crying for food."

"But haven't I got a kid, too?"

"If it suits you for him to die of hunger, that's all very well. That won't keep me, if we're still here to-morrow, from going to find the boss, and we can both tell him about it. We can't all stay here for the sake of that lady, may the devil fly away with her!"

"You're only a coward!" the woman exclaimed indignantly.

"I've got my kids, but I'd sooner they were under the ground than play such a dirty trick!"

"Everyone to his taste," the workman ended the discussion. "We'll see to-morrow."

Jane Blazon was overcome, stricken to the heart. So that was how they spoke about her openly, that was how these unhappy people thought of her, as the sole cause of their sufferings! The idea was intolerable. But what could she do to show them they were wrong?

Hour by hour, minute by minute, that day, the 5th of May, crept wearily to its end. The sun set. The night fell. For the third time since Tongané had set out, thick clouds covered the moon, and the darkness was profound. Would the negro take advantage of these favourable circumstances and give the long-awaited signal?

Although they no longer hoped, all eyes were fixed, as before, on that angle of the wall whence the signal was to be given. Seven, eight, half past eight, rang out from the Factory clock. They waited in vain.

A few minutes after half past eight a shudder ran through the anxious assembly. No, Tongané had not foresaken them! Above the wall of the Black quarter the signal had at last appeared!

They acted without losing an instant. On Camaret's instructions a strange-looking contrivance was brought to the top of the scaffolding. It was a cannon, a real cannon, though without wheels or gun-carriage, and though constructed of wood. Into the hollow of that strange bombard, made out of a tree-trunk, was placed a projectile; then a powerful jet of compressed air launched this silently into space.

It took with it a double hawser of steel fastened to a grapnel which, if all went well, would hook on to the crest of the wall of the slave's quarter.

The weight of the projectile, the degree of compression of the air, the pointing of the cannon, the shape and position of the grapnel, all had been carefully worked out by Camaret, who would not leave to anyone else the tasks of discharging this strange piece of artillery.

Silently the projectile soared over the quay, the river, the Merry Fellows' quarters, and fell into that of the Blacks. Had they succeeded and was the grapnel fast to the top of the wall?

Camaret gently moved the pulley over which the hawser passed. Soon it checked and resisted his efforts. Yes, the scheme had been crowned with success. Now an aerial roadway united the garrison to the slaves.

Along that road transport of the weapons at once began. First a packet of explosives was sent across, then four thousand knives, axes and pikes. By eleven the operation was complete. They all left the scaffold and, arming themselves with whatever came to hand, they formed up behind the great door. Massed in a compact group, the women in their midst, they waited for an opportune moment to intervene.

But someone was lacking from that group : a woman, Jane Blazon.

St. Bérain, Amédée Florence, Barsac and Dr. Châtonnay vainly shouted her name until the echoes rang, and vainly sought for her everywhere. They could not find her.

Aided by some of the good-hearted workmen, they renewed their efforts without any more success. The Factory was fruitlessly searched from end to end.

They had to yield to the evidence. Jane had disappeared.

CHAPTER XI

WHAT THERE WAS BEHIND THE DOOR

JANE BLAZON had certainly gone off, and in the easiest possible way. She simply went out without difficulty through the door, which she found merely bolted and not locked as usual. Enquiry showed that the man on duty at the cycloscope had seen her leaving the Factory but had not recognized her. His orders forbidding him to cause bloodshed except where absolutely necessary, he had not wanted to use one of the wasps against a solitary individual who, moreover, far from seeking to enter the Factory, was in fact leaving it.

The look-out's report showed that Jane, after leaving the Factory, had followed the quay upstream. Thus no illusion was possible; there could be no doubt that she had put into effect the plan which the others had opposed, and was most injudiciously going to give herself up to Harry Killer just at the very moment when her sacrifice was no longer needed.

The quay which downstream ended on the circular road was closed, upstream, by the Esplanade walls; this transformed it into a blind alley. Here, however, an armoured gate was let into the wall. This gate, normally shut, and to which Marcel Camaret and Harry Killer alone held the key, had been left open since hostilities had begun. Unless the Merry Fellows barred her way, therefore, Jane Blazon could have reached the Esplanade and followed it to the Palace.

It was in a moment of despair that she had taken flight. For everyone to believe that they were sacrificing themselves solely for her sake and accuse her of being the cause of all their distress, that thought horrified her, and she was no less horrified to feel herself hated by all these wretches whom she saw suffering around her. But suppose they were right? Suppose she were indeed the only booty which Harry Killer hoped to gain from the struggle? Were that possible, then

any delay would be criminal, and she blamed herself for
having so long hesitated to seek this chance of saving so many
of her fellows. And even if the garrison were mistaken, un-
likely though this seemed, in regarding their salvation as rest-
ing solely on her, did not her honour demand that she should
show them their mistake, even at the cost of her life?

Tongané's delay in giving the signal so anxiously looked for
had allowed time for her thoughts to dominate a mind rendered less lucid by hardships. So, at last, on the evening of
the 5th of May, she suddenly lost her head, and rushed to
carry out what she regarded as her duty.

Without noticing it, hardly aware of what she was doing,
she gently opened the door and slipped through it; then, after
silently closing the door, she set off towards the Palace, striving to hide against the wall so brightly lit by the Factory's
searchlights.

Like the look-out at the cycloscope, the Merry Fellows
posted on the exterior wall of the town, where the quay
crossed the circular road, had at once noticed her. But they
had not thought it their duty to open fire on a solitary shadow
which might in fact have something to do with their own
side.

So Jane arrived without difficulty on the Esplanade and
went on through the unlocked gate. Following the wall along
the bank of the Red River, she courageously came out on to
that broad space without troubling about the groups of the
Merry Fellows between which she had to pass. So startled
were they by her audacity that she covered the greater part
of the distance without being molested, and she was only
about twenty steps from the Palace when two men emerged
from one of the groups to challenge her.

These men had happened to see her, before the prisoners
escaped, moving freely about the Palace. When they recognized her, they uttered surprised exclamations; uncertain
about her object, uneasy because of the favour which their
Chief had shown her, and not knowing what to do, they not

merely let her pass without raising any objection but even
escorted her as far as the Palace, and opened the door to
admit her.

The moment she crossed the threshold, the door shut behind her. Whether she wished it or not she would henceforth
be in the power of Harry Killer, and without the slightest
hope that anyone could come to her aid.

In the Palace her arrival aroused the same surprise as on
the Esplanade. The black servant who admitted her hastened
to lead her to the Master. She followed him up the stairs,
along the galleries and the dark corridors, and at last into a
brilliantly lit room, which she at once recognized. It was the
Throne Room, as Amédée Florence facetiously called it, into
which the prisoners had been thrust for their only interview
with the despot of Blackland, and whose only furniture had
consisted of a table and an arm-chair.

The arm-chair was there still, and as before Harry Killer
was sprawled in it, behind a table loaded with bottles and
glasses. But arm-chair and table no longer formed the only
furniture. Nine other chairs had been brought in; one of these
was vacant, and in the others, eight brutal-looking men were
lounging and drinking. Harry Killer was carousing with his
Counsellors.

On seeing the girl framed in the doorway, these nine half-
drunken men roused themselves with grunts of surprise. Nothing could have taken them so much aback as this unexpected
appearance of one of the Factory garrison.

They jumped up, all shouting : "Miss Mornas !"

"Alone? . . ." asked Harry Killer. Leaning forward on the
table he threw an uneasy glance towards the corridor which
appeared behind the door as a dark oblong.

"Alone," Jane replied in a voice at once determined and
trembling; her legs were giving way under her, and she had
to lean against the doorpost.

For a few seconds the nine men, overcome with surprise,
gazed silently at the girl. For her to have come and to be there

alone was absolutely amazing. She, the focus of their gaze, felt increasingly confused, and she began very bitterly to regret her rashness.

"You've come from down there?" Harry Killer at last enquired thickly, pointing towards the Factory.

"Yes," Jane Blazon whispered.

"What have you come here for?"

His tone was less than amiable. Jane realized that the starving wretches in the Factory must have been mistaken when they regarded her as being solely responsible for their misfortunes. More than ever she feared that her sacrifice would do nothing to ease their burden.

"I've come to give myself up," she murmured, in spite of her deep humiliation as she realized the slight value they seemed to place on her sacrifice.

"Well! Well!" said Harry Killer sardonically; then, turning towards his companions, he added, "Leave us alone, comrades."

The eight Counsellors arose, all more or less unsteady on their feet. "That's all right, we'll leave you," said one of them, with a broad grin.

They were just reaching the door when Harry Killer halted them with a gesture and turned towards Jane Blazon: "I needn't ask what happened to Tchoumouki," he said, "I've found the bits! But what about the other one with him?"

"It wasn't we who killed Tchoumouki," Jane replied. "He died in the explosion, trying to blow up the heliplane. His comrade was wounded at the same time, and they're tending him in the Factory."

"Aha! . . ." said Harry Killer. "What about the heliplane?"

"Destroyed," answered Jane.

Harry Killer rubbed his hands with satisfaction, while his eight Counsellors disappeared. "So you've come to give yourself up, have you?" he asked, when he was alone with her. "And why are you giving yourself up?"

"To save the others," Jane replied courageously.

"Impossible!" exclaimed Harry Killer, with a chuckle. "So they've got to the end of their tether, have they?"

"Yes," Jane declared, lowering her eyes.

Filled with delight, Harry Killer poured out a large bumper of alcohol, which he swallowed at a single gulp. "Well?" he asked when he'd finished drinking.

"Some time ago," Jane murmured, her face red with shame, "you wanted me to be your wife. I agree, on condition that you let the others go."

"On condition! . . ." exclaimed Harry Killer in surprise. How do you fancy things are, child? As the folk in the Factory are played out, I shall have them to-morrow or the day after, and you into the bargain. It wasn't worth your while coming this evening—it only puts me a day ahead."

He got up and staggered towards her. "You've got cheek, to ask for conditions! . . ." he exclaimed. "Conditions for becoming my wife! Well, you'll be my wife when I want you to. And now, just how are you going to stop me? Wouldn't I like to know!"

He advanced towards Jane Blazon, who recoiled in terror, her hands stretched out before her. He was almost touching her. Soon, checked by the wall, she felt right in her face his alcohol-tainted breath.

"I can die, anyhow," she said.

"Die! . . ." repeated Harry Killer, as motionless as his shaking legs would allow. He was brought up short by the cold determination with which she uttered this word. "Die!" he repeated once more, scratching his chin indecisively.

A moment's silence, then another idea struck him. "Pah! . . . We'll see about that to-morrow. We shall soon come to an understanding, my girl! And meantime, let's make ourselves comfortable and happy."

Returning to his arm-chair he held out his glass. "Let's have a drink!" he said.

One glass followed another, and a quarter of an hour later

Harry Killer, already three parts drunk when Jane arrived, was snoring like a grampus.

So again the girl held at her mercy the brute who might well be her brother's murderer. She could have struck him to the heart, with the very dagger which had struck George Blazon. But what would be the good of that? Would it not, indeed, destroy the last vestige of the hope that she could bring any help to those whom she wanted to save?

For some time she waited, wrapped in thought, and her eyes fixed on the sleeping despot. Then a sudden pang assailed her. She was gripped by hunger, a cruel and imperious hunger.

For the moment she forgot her situation, the place where she found herself, and even Harry Killer himself; she forgot everything except her need for food. Eat, at all costs she must eat at once.

She carefully opened the door through which the eight Counsellors had made their exit, and in an adjacent room she saw a table covered with the remains of a meal. They must have been having a feast before winding up the evening in the Throne Room.

Jane rushed towards the table and picked up at random some fragments of food, which she quickly devoured. As she ate, life returned to her exhausted body; her heart sent the blood speeding through her arteries, and she regained her physical and moral energy.

Refreshed, she went back into the room where she had left Harry Killer. He was still asleep and raucously snoring.

She seated herself in front of him, waiting for him to awake.

A few minutes elapsed, then he moved and something rolled on to the floor. Stooping down, Jane picked up the object fallen from his pocket. It was a small key.

At this, memories crowded back into her mind. She remembered Harry Killer's regular exits, and how much she had wanted to know what it was he kept behind the door, whose lock was opened by this key which he always kept on him. And now chance had given her the means of satisfying her curiosity! The temptation was too great. She must take advantage of the opportunity, which was hardly likely to recur.

Moving very quietly, she reached the door through which Harry Killer was wont to vanish every day, and put the key into the lock. The door turned silently on its hinges. Behind it she found a landing from which a staircase led down to the lower floors. Having quietly pushed the door to without closing it, Jane tip-toed down the staircase, dimly lit by a gleam from below.

The room she had just left was on the second floor of the Palace. Yet, when she had gone down two floors she only came out on to another landing; below this was another stairway which must lead down to the basement. After a moment's hesitation, she went further down.

She came out at last into a sort of oblong vestibule, on the threshold of which she stopped abruptly. A negro was seated on guard in a recess, and at her approach he rose suddenly.

But she was quickly reassured. The warder seemed to have no hostile intention. On the other hand, he flattened himself respectfully against the wall to allow more room for his nocturnal visitor. She realized the cause for this unexpected deference when she recognized in this warder a member of the Black Guard. Like the Merry Fellows who had escorted her along the Esplanade, he had too often seen her moving freely about the Palace to have any doubts as to her influence over the Master.

With a determined step she went past him unopposed. But all was not over yet. Beyond the man there was a door.

Simulating a confidence which she did not feel, Jane put Harry Killer's key into the lock; it opened this as it had opened the other. She then found herself in a fairly long corridor, a mere extension of the vestibule she had just crossed, with a dozen or so doors opening in its walls to right and left.

All except one were wide open. Jane threw a glance into

the rooms they disclosed, and saw that these were nothing but cells, or rather dungeons, dark and airless, and furnished only with a table and a wretched apology for a bed. Otherwise they were empty, and nothing suggested that they had been occupied for some time.

There remained only the locked door. For the third time Jane tested the power of her key; like the two others the door opened without difficulty.

At first she could distinguish nothing within the dungeon which was plunged into profound darkness. Then, as her eyes gradually became accustomed to the dimness, she was able to make out in the gloom a confused heap, from which came the regular breathing of a sleeping man.

As if some supernatural power had warned her that she had unwittingly made an important discovery, Jane felt herself grow weak. Trembling, her heart throbbing, feeling lost and devoid of strength, she stood motionless on the dungeon's threshold, her ear and her eye seeking in vain to reach into the impenetrable darkness.

Then at last she remembered seeing just outside the door an electric switch. Without taking her eyes from the gloomy cell she succeeded in making use of this.

What was the astonishment she now felt—or rather the fear that assailed her!

If she had found, in that inner depth of the Blackland Palace, one of the men whom she had left in the Factory a few minutes before, or even if she had found her brother George Blazon, although she knew him to be dead ten years ago, she could hardly have been more taken aback.

Suddenly aroused by the switching on of the electric light, a man had sat erect on the wretched sleeping-place in one of the corners of the dungeon. Clothed in rags, whose holes disclosed a body covered with countless wounds and as thin as a skeleton, he tried painfully to stand up, while he turned towards the door eyes astare with fright.

Yet, in spite of the frightful evidences of long torture, in spite of his emaciated face, in spite of his beard and of his uncut hair, Jane could not be mistaken: she at once recognized the wretched prisoner.

Incredible, wonderful, was her recognition of the man who lay there in the depths of the Blackland dungeon. It was he whom six months before she had left peacefully at work in England. This human wreck, this martyr—it was Lewis Robert Blazon, it was her brother!

Panting, her eyes astare, Jane was momentarily unable to move and unable to speak.

"Lewis! . . ." she cried at last, hastening towards her hapless brother, who stammered in his bewilderment: "Jane! . . . You here! . . . Here!"

They threw themselves into one another's arms, and for some time, seized by convulsive sobs, they mingled their tears without being able to utter a word.

"Jane," murmured Lewis at last, "how could you have come to rescue me?"

"I'll tell you later," Jane answered. "But tell me about yourself first, Tell me how you got here."

"What do you think I can tell you?" exclaimed Lewis, with a gesture of despair. "I don't understand it myself. It was five months ago, on the 30th of November, when in my own office, I was knocked out by a violent blow on the back of the neck. When I recovered consciousness I was trussed up, gagged, and thrust into a chest. I've been carried about in a score of ways, like a parcel. Where am I? I don't know. Over more than four months I've never left this dungeon, and every day they lacerate my flesh with pincers, or sometimes with a whip. . . ."

"Oh! . . . Lewis! . . . Lewis!" groaned Jane, who was still sobbing. "But who torments you like that?"

"That's the worst of all," Lewis replied distressfully. "You could never imagine who it is that is guilty of these atrocities. It is. . . ."

He stopped abruptly. His outstretched arm indicated something in the corridor, and his eyes, his whole face, showed all the signs of extreme fear.

Jane looked in the direction towards which he was pointing. She turned pale, and her hand, which unobtrusively slid into her clothing, grasped the weapon she had found in the tomb at Koubo. His eyes bloodshot and his mouth, from which flowed a dribble of saliva, contorted into the snarl of a wild beast, fierce, terrifying, hideous—there stood Harry Killer.

CHAPTER XII

HARRY KILLER

"Harry Killer!" cried Jane.

"Harry Killer?" Lewis Blazon repeated, doubtfully, as he stared in amazement at his sister.

"Himself," growled Harry Killer in a raucous voice.

He took a pace forward. Pausing on the threshold of the open door, which his athletic figure completely filled, he leaned against the doorpost, his equilibrium still affected by the nights carousings.

"So this is what brought you here?" he stammered wrathfully. "Well, well, so mademoiselle has an assignment unbeknownst to her future husband!"

"Her husband?" repeated Lewis even more bewildered than before.

"Did you think I could be bamboozled so easily?" went on Harry Killer, advancing into the dungeon and stretching out his enormous hairy hands towards Jane.

But she was brandishing the weapon she had taken from her clothing: "Keep your distance!" she cried.

"Well! . . . Well! . . ." said Harry Killer sarcastically. "So the wasp has a sting!"

In spite of his sarcasm, he was prudent enough to stop. He stood there motionless, in the middle of the dungeon, his eyes fixed on the dagger with which Jane was menacing him.

Taking advantage of his indecision, the girl, leading her brother with her, had gone towards the door, thus cutting off the retreat of an adversary whom she regarded with fear.

"Yes, I have a weapon," she replied, trembling. "And what a weapon! I found this dagger in a grave . . . at Koubo!"

"At Koubo?" Lewis repeated. "Wasn't it there that George? . . ."

"Yes," said Jane, "it was at Koubo that George fell—it was there that he died, slain not by the bullets, but by this weapon

156

—and it bears a name engraved upon it : the name of the assassin, Killer."

Harry Killer had taken a pace backwards at that mention of the tragedy at Koubo. Pale, overcome, he was leaning against the dungeon wall, and looking at Jane as though terrified.

"Killer, did you say?" exclaimed Lewis. "But you're wrong, Jane. That isn't this man's name. He has another name, even worse than Killer another name which will not be new to you."

"Another name?"

"Yes. . . . You were too young when he left us to recognize him now, but you've often heard him talked about. When your mother married your father she had a son. That son is the very man whom you see here—it is your half-brother, William Ferney!"

This revelation had opposite effects on the other two.

While Jane, half-fainting, let fall her nerveless hand, William Ferney—who must now be allowed his rightful name— seemed to have regained his self-assurance. At the same time his drunkenness had vanished. He stood erect, and faced the little group formed by Jane and Lewis, towards whom he was darting looks alive with hatred and full of an implacable cruelty.

"Ah, so you are Jane Blazon," he said in menacing tones. Then he repeated, grinding his teeth, "So you are Jane Blazon!"

Then suddenly, all the evil sentiments which strangled him finding vent at once, he spoke, spoke so quickly that he had no time to put his words together. He spoke in short abrupt phrases, his chest heaving, his voice thick, his eyes flaming :

"Well, I'm glad ! . . . Yes, indeed, I'm very glad. . . . Well, so you went to Koubo ! . . . Yes, granted, it was I who killed him . . . your brother George . . . that fine fellow George . . . whom the Blazon family were so proud of ! . . . I even killed him twice . . . first in his soul . . . and then in his body . . .

and now I've got you here, the two of you . . . in my power, under my feet! You belong to me! . . . I can do what I like with you! . . ."

The words his throat emitted could hardy be understood. He was stammering, drunk with joy, exulting, triumphant.

"When I remember that I'd got one . . . and that the other came to me of her own accord! . . . It's too funny! . . ."

He took a step forward, while neither Jane nor Lewis, who were clutching one another, moved. Leaning towards them, he continued:

"You think you know a lot, don't you? But you don't know anything. . . . But I'm going to tell you everything . . . . Everything! . . . It will be a pleasure! Well, he drove me out, your father! . . . He can be very glad of that! . . . But only one thing mars my delight. . . . I want him to know . . . before he dies . . . whose hand struck those blows. . . . That hand . . . look at it . . . it was mine! . . ."

He advanced further. He was almost touching the brother and sister, who recoiled, terrified by this attack of insane ferocity.

"Well, they drove me out! What could I have done with the beggarly pittance they offered me? . . . I wanted gold, plenty of gold, mountains of gold! . . . I got it . . . gold . . . by the shovel-full . . . in heaps . . . without your help . . . without the help of anyone . . . all by myself! . . . And what did I do to get it? . . . Ha! . . . What the people of your sort call crimes. . . . I've robbed . . . killed . . . murdered . . . every . . . every crime . . . Ha!

"But gold wasn't enough for me. . . . My strongest motive was the hate I feel for you . . . for you all . . . the wretched House of Glenor! . . . That's why I came to Africa. . . . I trailed George Blazon's column. . . . I was taken to him. . . . I played a fine comedy . . . regret . . . repentance . . . remorse . . . I was a liar, a cheat, a hypocrite. . . . It was war, wasn't it? . . . The fool let himself be taken in. . . . He welcomed me with open arms. . . . I shared his tent, his table. . . . Ha! I took full ad-

vantage of his stupid confidence. . . . Every day a little more
powder in his food. . . . That powder? . . . What does that
matter? Opium . . . hashish . . . or something of the kind . . .
that's my business. . . . Go and find George Blazon. . . . A child,
a little helpless child.

"The leader? . . . Myself! . . . Then, what a triumph! . . .
The papers were full of it. . . . George Blazon goes insane . . .
George Blazon the murderer . . . George Blazon the traitor . . . .
That was all they talked about. . . . Who was it laughed, later
on, when he read the papers? . . . I think it was me. . . . But
let's get on. . . . One day the soldiers came. George Blazon
dead, that was good . . . dishonoured, that was better still. . . .
So I killed him to shut his mouth.

"Then I came on here, and I founded this city. . . . Not too
bad, was it, for somebody who was kicked out in disgrace?
Here, I'm the boss . . . the master, the king . . . the emperor
. . . I give orders, and the others obey. . . . Still, I wasn't quite
satisfied. . . . Your father still had a son and a daughter. That
wasn't to be borne. . . . First the son. . . . One day when I
wanted money I took his . . . and him into the bargain. . . .
Ha, ha! Knocked out, the son was . . . trussed up like a chicken,
the son was . . . stuffed into a trunk, the son was. . . . Then off
we go. . . . Trains, steamships, heliplanes, off we go! Right
down here . . . to me . . . in my kingdom! . . . And I shall kill
him . . . like the other . . . but not so quickly. . . slowly. . . day
after day! . . . And meanwhile . . . down there . . . in England
. . . the father . . . Oh, a noble lord! . . . and rich! . . . the
father knows that his son has vanished . . . taking the cash-box
with him. . . . Nicely worked out, all that, God damn my soul!

"But there's still the girl . . . my sister. . . . Ha, ha, my sister. . . . Now it's her turn. . . . What shall I do to her? . . . I've
thought about it. I've cudgelled my brains. . . . Good, she's
come here! . . . Here's my chance! . . . Not so long ago I was
going to make her my wife! . . . Just to torture her! . . . My
wife! . . . Not a bit of it! . . . The wife of the lowest of my
slaves . . . the vilest of my negroes!

"Then what will be left . . . for the old lord . . . in spite of all his titles and his wealth? . . . His two sons . . . one a traitor . . . one a thief. . . . His daughter? . . . Gone . . . vanished, nobody knows where. . . . And he . . . left alone . . . with his old-fashioned notions. . . . There's a fine ending for the House of Glenor!"

Uttered in a gasping voice, these frightful curses ended in nothing less than a howl.

William Ferney paused, completely out of breath, stifled with rage. His eyes were starting out of their sockets. He stretched towards his victims his clutching hands, ready to tear their hated flesh. He was no longer human. He was a homicidal maniac in the grip of lunacy, a ferocious beast, seeking only to destroy.

Alarmed more for him even than for themselves, Jane and Lewis Blazon gazed horror-struck at the madman. How could the human heart cherish so frightful a hatred?

"For to-night," the monster continued, when he had regained his breath, "I'm going to leave you together, as that seems to amuse you. But to-morrow. . . ."

The noise of an explosion, which certainly must have been great to reach the dungeon, suddenly drowned his voice. He stopped abruptly, surprised, uneasy, listening anxiously. . . .

The explosion was followed by several minutes of complete silence, then they heard a noise. . . . Cries, distant howlings, all the din of a frantic mob, mingled now and again with rifle or revolver shots. . . .

William Ferney was no longer thinking about Jane nor about Lewis Blazon. He was listening, trying to understand the meaning of the din.

The man from the Black Guard posted at the entrance to the dungeon suddenly rushed in, "Master," he cried, as though panic-stricken. "The town is on fire!"

Ferney gave vent to a frightful oath; then, contemptuously thrusting aside Jane and Lewis Blazon as they tried to bar his way, he dashed down the corridor and vanished.

The interruption had taken place so quickly that the brother and sister had not had time to comprehend it. In their bewilderment they had hardly noticed the explosion and the uproar which had freed them from their executioner. For an instant they failed to realize that they were alone. Still holding tightly on to one another, and overcome by the disgusting scene they had just witnessed, enfeebled by their recent sufferings, thinking of the old man who was dying in despair and shame, they were sobbing bitterly.

F

CHAPTER XIII

A NIGHT OF BLOODSHED

OVERWHELMED by the frightful experience they had just undergone, forgetting all except their own sufferings, Jane and Lewis Blazon stayed for some time huddled together. Then they gradually overcame their emotion; and at last, sighing deeply, they regained their awareness of the outside world.

What first struck them, in spite of the confused noise which rumbled around them, was a disquieting feeling of silence. In the corridor, still brightly lit by the electric lamps, was the peace of the grave. The Palace seemed to be dead. Outside, on the other hand, a tumultous din, the sound of firearms, an uproar which every minute increased in strength.

For a moment they listened attentively to these inexplicable sounds, then Jane suddenly realized their meaning. She turned towards her brother. "Can you walk?" she asked.

"I'll try," Lewis answered.

"Come along then," she told him.

The two were a pitiable sight as, the girl supporting a man worn out by four months of suffering, they left the dungeon, traversed the corridor, and arrived at the vestibule, where the guard had been waiting.

He had gone, and the vestibule was deserted.

They painfully climbed the staircase up to the third floor. Using the key she had taken from William Ferney, Jane opened the door at the top landing. Then, followed by Lewis, she entered the room, where shortly before she had left in his drunken stupor the monstrous lunatic in whom she had then failed to recognize her half-brother.

Like the vestibule below, the room was empty, but nothing else had changed since she left it. Ferney's arm-chair still stood behind the table, laden with its glasses and bottles, and the nine other chairs were still ranged in a semi-circle facing it.

After leading her brother to a seat, for his legs were giving way beneath him, Jane realized the strangeness of the situation in which they found themselves. Why this solitude, and why this silence? What had become of their executioner?

Giving way to a sudden impulse, she ventured to leave Lewis, and courageously went out into the Palace, exploring it in every direction.

She began with the ground floor, and did not leave a corner uninvestigated. Going past the outer door, one glance showed her that it had been carefully shut. Throughout the ground floor she saw nobody; all its inner doors stood wide open, just as its inhabitants had left them. With increasing astonishment she traversed the other floors and found them equally deserted. However incredible this might be, the palace seemed to be empty.

The floors having been investigated, there remained only the central tower and the terrace it commanded. At the foot of the staircase leading up to this, Jane paused thoughtfully for a moment, then she slowly began the ascent.

No, the Palace was not completely deserted, as she had thought. When she approached the top of the staircase, the sound of voices came to her from outside. Very carefully she climbed the topmost steps; then, sheltered in the gloom, she looked out on the terrace lit by the distant glow of the Factory searchlights.

There the whole population of the Palace was assembled. Shuddering with horror, Jane recognized William Ferney, as well as the eight Counsellors whom she had seen with him shortly before. Further on, in two groups, were some of the Black Guard and the nine negro servants.

Leaning over the parapet, they seemed to be pointing to something in the distance, and they were exchanging cries rather than words, and accompanying them with gestures. What could be happening to enrage them so much?

Suddenly Ferney stood erect and shouted an order at the top of his voice; then, followed by the others, he made for the stairway on whose top steps Jane was sheltering. As she saw, they were armed each with two revolvers strapped to his belt and wrathfully gripping a rifle.

Another second, and her hiding-place would be discovered. Then what would become of her in the hands of these violent men? She was lost.

Looking about her, unconsciously seeking for some impossible means of escape, her eyes suddenly fell on a door at the top of the stairway, shutting it off from the terrace. To see and to slam that door, which clanged noisily, were one and the same action. Jane's position was at once completely changed—changed by an instinctive action which she could hardly remember making.

Cries of fury and horrible oaths responded from outside. She had hardly time to shoot the last bolts before the men on the terrace were battering violently with their rifle-butts on this unexpected obstacle which now barred their way.

Terrified by these vociferations, by these repeated blows, by all the din, Jane stayed where she was, trembling and unable to move. She kept her eyes fixed on the door, every minute expecting it to give way under the attack of these dreadful foes.

But the barrier did not fall; it did not seem to be so much as shaken by the furious blows showered upon it. Gradually Jane recovered her self-control: she realized that, like the outer doors of Factory and Palace, this door was made of thick armour-plating able to defy all attacks. There was no reason to fear that Ferney would be able to break it down with the weak forces at his command.

Reassured, she was returning to her brother when she noticed that the stairway, between the bottom floor of the Palace and the terrace, could be barred by five similar doors, Ferney had foreseen everything needed to guard against a surprise attack. His Palace was divided into a number of sections separated by these barriers, which would need to be stormed one after another. Now these precautions could be turned against himself.

Jane bolted these five doors as she had bolted the topmost, and went down to the ground floor.

The Palace windows were protected by massive grilles, as well as by thick metal shutters. Without waiting a moment she went from floor to floor closing all these shutters, down to the very last.

Where did she get the strength to move those massive plates? She worked feverishly and almost unconsciously, as though she were sleep-walking, but skilfully and quickly. In an hour the task was finished. She was now at the heart of an impregnable block of masonry and steel.

It was only then that she realized how weary she was, her legs beginning to give way under her. Worn out, and her hands bloodstained, she could scarcely get back to her brother.

"Whatever is the matter?" he asked anxiously, alarmed to see her in such a state.

When she had regained her breath she explained what she had done. "Now we are masters of the Palace," she ended triumphantly.

"Isn't there any other way out besides that stair?" enquired her brother, who could hardly believe in such a master-stroke.

"There's no other way," Jane declared. "I'm certain of that. William is blockaded on the terrace, and I defy him to get away."

"But why were they up there together?" Lewis wanted to know. "Whatever can have happened?"

But that was something which Jane did not understand. Of all the preparations for defending the Factory she had seen nothing. But it would be easy to find out, by simply glancing outside. Together they climbed to the upper floor, above which was only the terrace, and opened a chink in one of the shutters which Jane had just closed.

Then they could realize the dismay of William Ferney and his companions. Though at their feet the Esplanade lay dark and silent, brilliant lights and a terrible uproar could be made out on the right bank of the Red River. All the huts of the negroes were ablaze. The centre part of the town, the slaves' quarter, was nothing but an inferno.

The fire was similarly raging among the dwellings of the Civil Body, and up and down stream the extremities of the Merry Fellows' quarter was also beginning to burn.

In the rest of that quarter not yet reached by the fire a frightful din could be heard : cries, oaths, appeals for mercy, confused howlings, mingled with the incessant crackle of the fusilade.

"That must be Tongané," said Jane. "The slaves are in revolt."

"The slaves. . . . Tongané? . . ." Lewis repeated; the words had no meaning for him.

His sister explained the organization of Blackland, so far as she understood it herself. She summed up briefly how she had found herself in the town, and the events which had led to their being taken prisoner. She told him why she had undertaken that journey, how she had succeeded in demonstrating the innocence—by now certain—of their brother George, and how, after having linked up with the Mission commanded by le Député Barsac, she had been abducted along with its remnants.

She pointed out, beyond the Esplanade, the Factory lit up by the blaze of its searchlights, and she told him about her companions who, except for the negro Tongané, were still sheltered within it. As for Tongané, it was he who had undertaken to rouse the coloured people of Blackland, and the sight which met their eyes proved that he had succeeded. But she had not had the patience to wait, and so she had fled alone, that very evening, in the hope of saving the rest of the garrison. It was thus that she had reached her unfortunate brother. Meantime Tongané had evidently given the pre-arranged signal, the weapons sent to him, and the revolt unleashed. No doubt William Ferney and his companions had been about to join in the fight when she had so brusquely slammed the door in their face.

"And now what are we going to do?" asked Lewis.

"Wait," replied Jane. "The slaves won't know us, and in all the confusion they won't be able to distinguish between us and anyone else. Besides, we couldn't give them much help—we haven't any weapons."

Lewis having very reasonably pointed out that it would be useful to have them, Jane made another tour of the Palace. The harvest she reaped was not over-plentiful. All the weapons, except the ones their owners had on them, were stored in the tower above the terrace, and the most she could find were one solitary rifle and two revolvers, with a handful of cartridges.

When she returned with them, the situation had completely changed. The negroes had broken out and invaded the Esplanade, on which they were swarming in thousands. In an instant they had stormed the barracks of the Black Guard, whose members they had massacred on the spot and the shelters of the forty heliplanes, from which jets of flame were soon leaping. Drunk with pillage and blood, frantic, they were now taking vengeance for their protracted sufferings, and everything showed that their rage would be satisfied only by the total destruction of the town and the slaughter of the last of its inhabitants.

Watching this spectacle, William Ferney must have been foaming with impotent rage. He could be heard howling and shouting, although the words he was using could not be made out. From the terrace came the crackle of a continual fusillade, and the bullets, striking into the swarming mob of negroes, were finding many victims.

But the others seemed heedless of this. After burning the quarters of the Black Guard and the heliplane shelters, whose flames were lighting up the Esplanade like gigantic torches, they were attacking the Palace itself and striving, so far vainly, to break down its doors with anything that came to hand.

They were still doing this when sudden bursts of fire sounded from the Red River bank. Having at last succeeded in closing their ranks, the Merry Fellows had crossed the bridge;

deploying on the Esplanade, they were firing at random into the mob. Soon hundreds of bodies were littering the ground.

The blacks, clamouring fiercely, were hurling themselves at these new adversaries. For some minutes it was an atrocious battle, an indescribable slaughter. Not having firearms, the negroes fought hand to hand, wielding their axes, their knives, their pikes, and in the last resort using their teeth. The Merry Fellows replied with bayonet thrusts and shots delivered at point-blank range.

The result of the conflict could not long remain in doubt. Superiority in weapons was bound to triumph over that in numbers. Hesitation soon appeared in the depleted ranks of the negroes, they recoiled, and soon they were fleeing towards the river bank, leaving the Esplanade to the conquerors.

These pursued them hotly in the hope of saving the centre of the Merry Fellows' quarter, which the fire had not yet reached.

At the very moment when they were crossing the bridge, a tremendous explosion roared out. From their vantage-point in the Palace, Jane and Lewis could see that it had occurred some distance away, in the remotest part of the Civil Body's quarter. By the light of the fires now raging everywhere, they saw too that part of that quarter and a long stretch of the exterior wall had just been blown up.

Whatever the cause of the explosion, its most obvious result was to open a way for the negroes to reach the open country. Through the breach thus formed the slaves were seeking refuge and escape from their enemies in the fields and the surrounding undergrowth.

Within a quarter of an hour their pursuers withdrew across the Red River and returned to the Esplanade. Not merely had they no longer any enemies confronting them, they were themselves terror-stricken by further explosions following close on the first.

What was the cause of these explosions? Nobody could say. It was however clear that they were occurring not at random but were deliberately planned. The first had taken place on the boundary of the town, in the part of the Civil Body's quarter most remote from the Palace.

Five minutes later two others could be heard to its right and left. Then, after another interval of five minutes, two others sounded nearer the river, but still in the Civil Body's quarter.

It was then that the Merry Fellows who had been following close on the heels of the slaves sought refuge on the Esplanade.

From that time onwards the inexplicable explosions occurred at regular intervals of about half an hour. Every thirty minutes a further uproar was heard, and another section of the Civil Body's quarter was reduced to rubble.

Huddled together on the Esplanade, the white population of Blackland, or at any rate all that remained of it, looked on dazed at these inexplicable happenings. It seemed indeed that a superior and formidable power had undertaken the methodical destruction of the town.

The bandits, formerly so courageous when dealing with those weaker than themselves, were now trembling with fear. Thrusting against the Palace, they strove in vain to break down its door, and they howled execrations against William Ferney, whom they could see on the terrace without understanding why he seemed to have forsaken them. For his part, he was wearing himself out making gestures which they could not interpret, and shouting words which were drowned in the deafening uproar.

Thus the night ended. Day as it broke revealed a frightful scene. The surface of the Esplanade was literally strewn with corpses, to the total of several hundred, blacks and whites mingled together. If the latter had gained the victory, they had paid dearly for it. Of the eight hundred odd men whom yesterday had dwelt in the Civil Body's and the Merry Fellows' quarters, scarcely four hundred remained unscathed. The others had perished as much at the beginning of the revolt, during the first surprise, as on the Esplanade itself when the revolt was over.

As for the slaves, Jane and Lewis could see, from their lofty viewpoint, that they were scattered about the surrounding country. Many were going away. Some were setting off westwards, making straight for the Niger, from which they were separated by an ocean of sand. How many of them would succeed in completing the journey, without water, without food, without weapons? Others, preferring a longer but safer route, were following the course of the Red River, and disappearing towards the south-west.

But the majority of them could not make up their minds to leave Blackland. They could be seen scattered in groups about the fields, gazing stupidly at the town, from which dense columns of smoke were rising, and which the series of explosions was steadily transforming into a heap of ruins.

At that moment a violent explosion sounded on the terrace of the Palace itself. Then, blow after blow, others followed it, the last being followed by a thunderous crash.

Without leaving the window whose partly-drawn shutters had enabled them to watch these dramatic events, Lewis grasped his sister's hand and questioned her with an anxious gaze.

"That's William," she explained, knowing too much about the build of the Palace not to understand the meaning of the explosions. "Now he's trying to blow down the terrace door with cannon-shots."

Jane spoke very calmly. She was watching the position and realizing its significance quite coolly.

"But then," cried Lewis, "they'll be coming down?" He grasped one of the revolvers his sister had found. "We'd better die rather than fall into their hands!"

Jane stopped him with a gesture. "They're not here yet," she said calmly. "There are five other doors like it, and they're placed, especially the three last, so that a cannon couldn't possibly be levelled against them."

As if to prove her right, the explosions had ceased. A heavy rumbling they could hear on the terrace, accompanied by

furious shouts, told them that William Ferney and his companions were striving to bring their cannon to bear against the
second door, and that the operation was not without difficulty.

Soon, moreover, their work was interrupted. Another incident which had just taken place must have attracted their
attention, just as it had that of Lewis and Jane Blazon.

The periodical explosions had now culminated in another
even more violent and even more destructive than its predecessors. The destructive power which had caused them was now
attacking the left bank of the stream, and it was the Factory
garden itself which was soaring towards the skies in a burst of
earth and stones. When the smoke had cleared away, it could
be seen that the garden had been destroyed for much of its
length, and that a small portion of the Factory itself had
collapsed.

The dust of the explosion was still hanging in the air when
a crowd could be seen hastening through the widely-opened
Factory door down on to the quay. Jane recognized them at
once : they were her companions in captivity, as well as Camaret's workmen, formed up in a compact body with the women
and children at its centre. Why were these unfortunate
wretches leaving their shelter and making for the Esplanade,
where they were sure to encounter the Merry Fellows, still
beating furiously but vainly against the Palace door?

The Merry Fellows could not see these new adversaries, who
were shut off from their view by the Esplanade wall. But William Ferney, who could see over the wall from his position on
the terrace, had noticed them and was pointing them out.

His gestures were not understood. The crowd emerging from
the Factory reached the door connecting the Esplanade with
the quay and passed through it.

When the Merry Fellows saw them, they gave vent to a
storm of howls. Breaking off their useless efforts, they seized
their weapons and dashed upon the newcomers.

But it was no longer with negroes that they had to contend.
Armed with anything which came to hand, one with a black-

smith's hammer, another with a pair of tongs, yet another with
a crude iron bar, the men from the Factory likewise dashed
upon them. The struggle was terrible, and the air was filled
with a deafening clamour. Streams of blood reddened the soil
of the Esplanade, already strewn with the bodies of those who
had fallen during the night.

Covering her eyes with her hands, Jane strove not to see that
horrible sight. How many among the combatants were her
friends! She trembled for Barsac, for Amédée Florence, for
kind-hearted Dr. Châtonnay, and especially for her dearly-
loved St. Bérain.

But howls even more violent suddenly burst forth.

Superiority of numbers and weapons was gaining the day.
The column from the Factory was cut in two. One half was
retreating towards the quay, defending its ground step by step,
while the other was being driven towards the Palace.

The latter, at least, could have no hope of escape. Hemmed
in against the wall, they had not only to face the Merry Fellows; from on the terrace William Ferney and his men could
open fire without risk to themselves upon these wretches from
whom even flight was debarred. . . .

Suddenly these gave a shout of joy. The door against which
they had been driven had suddenly been flung open behind
them, and upon its threshold had appeared Jane Blazon. Pursued by their enemies, they took refuge in the Palace, while
Jane and Lewis covered their retreat with rifle and revolver
shots.

Bewildered by this intervention which none of them could
understand, the Merry Fellows hesitated for a moment. When,
recovering from their surprise, they renewed the attack, it was
too late. The door had again been shut and was defying all
their efforts.

CHAPTER XIV

THE END OF BLACKLAND

WHEN the door had been firmly closed, the first task was to attend to the wounded, of whom there were many. Aided by Amédée Florence, himself slightly injured, and like Barsac, forced by an ironical fate to seek refuge in the lair of their implacable enemy, Jane Blazon lavished attention on them.

First-aid given, another task now devolved upon her. She had to feed the unhappy wretches who for several days had endured the pangs of hunger. But could she do this, and did the Palace contain enough food to satisfy so many mouths?

The quantity she was able to find, after having searched each of the floors, provided at most a very scanty meal. So the situation was still very grave, and its inevitable outcome seemed to have been postponed only for a few hours.

By the time these varied tasks had been accomplished, it was eleven in the morning. Meanwhile the explosions were continuing outside, and from the Esplanade there could still be heard the noise of the Merry Fellows who every now and again made another of their vain attacks on the door, while from the terrace came the outcries of William Ferney and his companions. As the survivors grew accustomed to this, they ended by paying no further attention to the uproar; confident that their stronghold was almost impregnable, they troubled less and less about its besiegers' fury.

As soon as she had leisure, Jane asked Amédée Florence why they had left the shelter of the Factory to venture so disadvantageously on to the Esplanade, and the reporter told her all that had occurred since she left them.

He explained how a little after half past eight, when Tongané had given the long-awaited signal, Marcel Camaret had, unknown to Blackland's other inhabitants, despatched to the central quarter several dynamite cartridges and a generous supply of weapons. This preliminary operation having been

173

completed towards eleven, the garrison had formed up ready
to take their part in the forthcoming struggle. It was then that
have been overcome by anxiety.

Amédée Florence described St. Bérain's despair : if the poor
fellow had survived the struggle, by now he must certainly
have been overcome by anxiety.

Half an hour after the weapons had been despatched, a
tremendous explosion was heard. Tongané had just blown up
one of the gates of the black quarter, whose huts had caught
fire, and to judge by the cries which followed, the slaves were
attacking and massacring the Civil Body.

Jane knew the rest. She knew that the negroes, after making
their way on to the Esplanade, had been so quickly repulsed
that there was no time to go to their aid. Her friends had made
their way out of the Factory but they had had to retire fighting, for by the time they arrived most of the blacks had
already been driven off the Esplanade.

Obliged to retire into the Factory, the garrison had passed
an anxious night. This check to the slaves' revolt made them
doubt whether this would be the end of Harry Killer. Like Jane
herself they too had listened to the series of explosions now de-
stroying the town without being able to explain them. It was at
last clear that they were the work of Marcel Camaret, who by
this time had gone completely insane.

Brilliant inventor though he undoubtedly was, Camaret had
always been at least on the verge of madness, as was shown
by anomalies in his behaviour inconsistent with a sane and well-
balanced intelligence. The incidents which had crowded on
him during the last month had ended by driving him out of
his mind.

The first shock had come from the disclosures made by
Harry Killer's captives when they had sought refuge in the
Factory. The second, and much more violent, had been given
by Daniel Frasne. Now that he realized the truth, Camaret had
every day lapsed further into madness. Jane recalled how often
since then he had shut himself up in his own quarters, and

how gloomy and preoccupied was his appearance whenever he roamed about the workshops.

Sending off the weapons to Tongané had been his last lucid action. When the explosion occurred, above all when the flames first rose from the quarters of the slaves and the Civil Body, those around him had seen him suddenly turn pale and hold his hand to his throat as though he were stifling. At the same time, he mumbled some words difficult to hear but easy to understand as he softly repeated : "The death of my work ! . . . The death of my work !"

For some time, perhaps a quarter of an hour, Marcel Camaret, anxiously watched by those around him had repeated these words and had turned his head restlessly from side to side. Then, suddenly, standing erect and smiting his breast, he had cried : "God has condemned Blackland ! . . ."

To judge by the gesture which accompanied that condemnation, by "God" he simply meant himself.

Before anyone had time to stop him, he had dashed away, continually exclaiming in a voice unrecognizably harsh : "God has condemned Blackland ! . . . God has condemned Blackland !"

He had taken refuge in the tower, closing all the doors behind him as he climbed the stairs. Its defensive works resembled those of the Palace, so it was as impossible for his friends to reach him as it was for Harry Killer to leave the terrace. As Camaret made his way upwards his voice could be faintly heard repeating, "God has condemned Blackland. . . . God has condemned Blackland."

The first explosion had followed almost at once.

Led by Rigaud, aghast at seeing the brilliant leader he loved in such a state, several of the workmen, in spite of their weakness, had dashed into the Factory and attempted to isolate the tower by cutting off its supply of electricity. But it was self-contained, for it had its own reserve supply as well as the generators driven by liquid air, so the explosions had not ceased. But when the wasps, forsaking their protective circling, had fallen into the Factory moat, it was plainly necessary to restore the current to Camaret. Insane though he was, he must have known quite clearly what he was about, for he again put those defensive weapons into action.

After a night of continual anxiety, the engineer had appeared on the platform of the tower. From that vantage point he had delivered a long discourse, of which only a few scattered words could be made out. Some of them, "Divine wrath," "fire from heaven," "complete destruction," had been enough to prove that his madness showed no signs of leaving him. At the end of his speech he had cried : "Fly! . . . Fly one and all!" in a voice loud enough to be heard all over the Factory. Then he had retired into the tower, whence he had not since emerged.

Immediately afterwards had come the first of the explosions on the left bank. This explosion, taking place in the Factory itself, had stricken its occupants with fear. At the risk of being slaughtered, and having nothing to choose but two ways of dying, they had made up their minds to attempt a sortie.

Unfortunately, when they emerged on the Esplanade they found themselves facing the Merry Fellows, who had previously been out of sight behind the wall. After suffering a number of casualties, the refugees had divided into two sections. Some, as already described, found a shelter in the lair of Harry Killer himself. The others were driven back on to the quay, but managed to barricade themselves by shutting the gate between this and the Esplanade.

This group were visible from the Palace. Daring neither to attempt another attack whose futility was obvious, nor to retire into the Factory, itself now at the mercy of a madman's whim, half-starved and their nerves shattered, they stayed in the open. Some had fallen to the ground, and all were exposed to an enemy who could either open fire on them from the other bank of the river or from the top of the Palace, or attack them in the rear along the circular road.

Jane was relieved to see that among them were St. Bérain and Dr. Châtonnay. So none of her friends had so far perished, and above all the relative whom she held so dear was still alive.

Hardly had she received this reassurance when heavy blows sounded from the upper floors of the Palace. These obviously came from the terrace, where its occupants were striving to tear up the paving. But this was solidly laid and resisted staunchly.

If William Ferney and his comrades, who must also have been short of food, had not been weakened by their privations they would soon have succeeded. A little after six in the evening, indeed, the terrace floor had been ripped up and the third floor had to be evacuated.

The garrison took refuge on the second floor, not forgetting to shut the armoured doors behind them, and there they waited.

Jane took advantage of the pause to tell Barsac and Amédée Florence about her own adventures since she had left the Factory. She explained the affairs of her family, and after relating how her brother Lewis had been so audaciously kidnapped and imprisoned, she told them of the sad discovery they had made, that Harry Killer was her own half-brother, William Ferney. If fate decided that she was not herself to return to England, Amédée Florence and Barsac could then be advocates for George and Lewis Blazon, accused of crimes which they had not committed.

Towards seven in the evening, the ceiling of the second storey began to give way under the blows rained upon it. William Ferney and his henchmen, after the pause which their weariness demanded, had again set to work. The refugees had to go further down.

To break this floor down would take as much effort as before. Until two in the morning, blows resounded throughout the Palace. Then came a silence of two hours, which William Ferney spent in descending to the second floor and in again seeking the rest he found more and more necessary.

The blows were not heard again, this time on the ceiling of the first floor, until about four in the morning. Without waiting for the ceiling to come down, the refugees sought shelter on the ground floor, but not without barring the way, as before, with armoured doors which nobody was going even to try to break down.

This was the last stronghold they could find. When William Ferney had got through the two ceilings which still separated him from themselves, when the rifle-barrels appeared over their heads, they would either have to seek refuge in the subterranean dungeons or else to retreat and keep retreating until they would at last be brought up against the outside wall of the Palace. Nothing would then be left for them but to die.

While William Ferney was striving to break down the last but one of the obstacles which barred his way, the sun rose in a cloudless sky. The extent of the destruction could then be realized : whatever happened, the despot of Blackland would henceforth reign over nothing but ruins.

The town was completely destroyed. Two houses alone were still standing, in the centre of the Merry Fellows' quarter, just opposite the Palace. A few minutes after sunrise these two collapsed in their turn, thus completing the total destruction on the right bank.

Far from ceasing, the explosions now followed more quickly than ever. Marcel Camaret was attacking the left bank, and now it was the turn of the Factory to collapse in ruins. Yet he was very skilfully directing the work of destruction. If he was overthrowing the workmen's houses, the workshops, the reserve stores, little by little, bit by bit, as though he wanted to maks his pleasure last as long as possible, he took care not to touch its vital parts, where the machines produced the energy of which he was making so terrible a use.

To the first explosion on the left bank, the Merry Fellows on the Esplanade, who during the night had kept fairly quiet and seemed to have given up their fruitless attacks on the door, replied by making a loud uproar and hurling themselves anew against the Palace.

Their determination was bewildering. Why were they so obstinate? Now that Blackland no longer existed, what did they hope to achieve? Would they not do better to leave this dead city and to try to reach the Niger?

A few words spoken outside, and overheard beyond the door, explained their conduct. They no longer aimed at rescuing their leader, whom they accused of betraying them; and their object was to escape from this desolation. First, however, they wanted to seize the treasure which they believed Harry Killer had stored in his Palace. When they had shared this out, they would lose no time in packing off and seeking their fortune under other skies.

The refugees would have been only too ready to give them that satisfaction. Unfortunately they did not know where the former despot of Blackland kept his secret hoard, if there were such a thing, and so they could not so easily rid themselves of their enemies.

But for the explosions which could be heard with growing frequency from the direction of the Factory, the position remained unaltered until nine. William Ferney was still trying to break through the ceiling of the first floor while the Merry Fellows continued to thunder against the door, which they found no less an obstacle.

But at the last moment they changed their tactics. Ceasing to exhaust themselves in vain on the door itself, they started to attack the masonry around it. For an hour their tools could be heard scraping against the stone, and then a loud explosion sent fragments flying from the lower part of the wall. They had been astute enough to bore a cavity; then, with powder from their cartridges, they were blowing up the obstacle they could not break down.

Though the door was still holding, it had been badly shaken, and a second explosion would certainly overthrow it. Already rifle barrels were appearing menacingly through the hole blasted in the wall.

The refugees had to leave the vestibule and to shelter in the farthest part of the Palace, while the Merry Fellows were boring a hole for their second mine.

Almost at the same moment, a noise of falling debris showed that the third of the ceilings had just given way. A few minutes later the refugees could hear footsteps on the first floor, while heavy blows sounded just above their heads.

The situation was certainly getting desperate. Outside were three or four hundred Merry Fellows who, within half an hour, would force their way in. Above, a score of determined bandits who, perhaps within the same time, would open fire through the ceiling of the ground floor. The refugees could not even try to contend with such a fate. Jane and Lewis Blazon, Amédée Florence and Barsac, sought vainly to reassure them. Sprawled on the floor, the unhappy wretches waited resignedly for the blow which would strike them down.

But the whole situation was suddenly changed. The Merry Fellows and William Ferney simultaneously interrupted their work. An explosion, which could not be confused with any of those still resounding nearby, had suddenly rung out and was re-echoing in every direction through the Palace. This explosion, which sounded like cannon-fire, was followed by several others, and within a few minutes a long stretch of the south-east wall, between the Esplanade and the open country, had suddenly collapsed.

A tumult of horrible oaths burst from the Merry Fellows as some of them gazed out through the newly-made breach. What they saw seemed to be not at all to their liking, for they began to gesticulate like madmen, and to argue wildly with their companions. Soon, while William Ferney, giving up his efforts to reach the ground floor, was hastening back to the top of the tower, they were rushing in a disorderly mob towards the other bank. Racing, jostling together in an inexplicable panic, they were striving to reach it when another explosion, costing the lives of about fifty of them, destroyed both the Castle and the Garden Bridges. All communication now being cut off with the right bank, the survivors threw themselves without hesitation into the water and swam across the river.

In a moment the Esplanade was deserted and, but for the

explosions still taking place at regular intervals, a deep silence
had followed the din. The astounded refugees were at a loss
what to do, when suddenly there came the collapse of a corner
of the Palace itself. Marcel Camaret was crowning his work
of destruction by starting to make the place uninhabitable.
They would have to escape.

They dashed out on to the Esplanade, and, anxious to know
what had caused the Merry Fellows to panic, they too hastened
towards the breach in the exterior wall. They had not yet
reached it when the notes of a bugle resounded from its far
side.

Unable to believe in the rescue which that bugle proclaimed,
they stopped irresolute, like their comrades who had previously
taken refuge on the quay, and who now came up at almost the
same moment.

It was thus that Captain Marcenay found them—for it was
he whose intervention had been announced by the roar of the
cannon and the notes of the bugle. There they were grouped
together in the middle of the Esplanade, pale, haggard, weak,
trembling with fatigue and hunger.

When the Tirailleurs appeared in the breach, the refugees
tried to go to meet them, but so overcome were they with
weakness and emotion that all they could do was to extend
their arms towards their rescuers; several, indeed, dropped
unconscious on the ground.

Such was the sad spectacle which greeted the eyes of Captain Marcenay as, at the head of his men, he reached the
Esplanade. Beyond the river a vast expanse of ruins, from
which rose columns of smoke. To right and left, two impressive structures partly shattered, but each dominated by a
tower which still remained intact. Immediately before him a
great open place littered with several hundred dead bodies,
and in the midst of them a huddled group of people from
whom came groans and cries of pain.

It was towards that group that Captain Marcenay advanced, as it was there alone that he could find any survivors.

And would he have the joy of finding the one he sought for, the one whom above all others he wished to rescue?

He was quickly reassured. On seeing the Captain, Jane Blazon, with a sudden burst of energy, had regained her feet and staggered towards him. He could hardly recognize in this poor creature, her face pale, her cheeks fallen in, her eyes shining with fever, the girl whom he had left, less than three months before, radiant in her health and strength. He hastened towards her just in time to catch her as she fainted in his arms.

While he was trying to restore her, two terrible explosions shook the earth on each side of the Esplanade. The Factory and the Palace had collapsed at once. Alone above their ruins stood the two towers, tall, massive, intact.

On top of that of the Palace could be seen William Ferney, the eight Counsellors, the nine negro servants and five men of the Black Guard. Twenty-three in all, they were leaning over the parapet and seemed to be appealing for help.

On the other tower was only one man. Three separate times he strode round the platform, addressing the distant horizon in an incomprehensible tirade accompanied by wild gestures. He must however have been shouting, for, although he was so far away, a few of his utterances could be caught; twice they rang out clearly: "Accursed. . . . Accursed be Blackland!"

William Ferney must also have heard them for he suddenly stamped with fury, seized a rifle, and fired at random towards the Factory tower, about four hundred yards away.

Rather by sheer chance than by judgment, the bullet found its mark. Marcel Camaret clapped his hand to his chest and staggered into the tower.

Almost at once there came a double explosion, even more violent than any of the others, and the two towers simultaneously collapsed. The one burying in its ruins William Ferney and his companions and the other Marcel Camaret, they fell with an appalling crash.

The terrible uproar was followed by a deep silence. Horror-struck, the survivors of the catastrophe were still gazing when there was nothing to see and listening when there was nothing to hear.

Everything was over. Blackland, completely destroyed by the man who had created it, was now only ruin and desolation. Of the magnificent but ill-fated achievements of Marcel Camaret there remained nothing.

CHAPTER XV

CONCLUSION

THUS perished Marcel Camaret and William Ferney, alias Harry Killer. Thus perished at the same time that astonishing city of Blackland, which had flourished unknown to the world. And with it perished the marvellous inventions it contained.

Of the town and its contents nothing remained but a heap of ruins, soon to vanish under a shroud of sand. The clouds ceased to shed their life-giving rain, the Red River ran dry and became a barren *oued* unmoistened by even a drop of water, the fields dried up, and the desert, reconquering its realm, advanced to the attack of that human creation, whose last vestige soon disappeared.

At the behest of its creator, Camaret's work was dead, and nothing would hand down to the ages the name of that brilliant but unbalanced inventor.

Captain Marcenay did everything possible to curtail his stay in this desolation. Over a month elapsed, however, before he could set out homewards. He had to inter the dead, several hundred in number, to tend the wounded, to wait until they were able to endure the journey, and to allow time for strength to return to those whom he had rescued at the last moment.

Several among the former personnel of Blackland would never again see their native country. A score of workmen, three women and two children were dead, fallen beneath the blows of the Merry Fellows.

Yet fate had protected the members—official and officious—of the Barsac Mission. Except for Amédée Florence, who had been slightly wounded, they had all come off scot-free. This also applied to Tongané and Malik, who had resumed the course of their idyll, which consisted in exchanging hearty slaps and grinning at each other for all they were worth.

While those who he had saved were recovering from the trials they had endured, while the wounds were healing, Captain Marcenay rounded up the scattered population of Black-land. Those of the whites who resisted arrest were soon brought to reason by a bullet, and the others were fettered, their fate to be finally decided by the law. The one-time slaves were gradually assembled and reassured. Taken back to the Niger, they were allowed to disperse, and they all succeeded in returning to their own villages and their relatives.

It was not until the 10th of June that the column could get into motion, well provided with food found plentifully among the ruins of the town and in the surrounding country. A few of the wounded, those most seriously injured, were not yet able to walk and had to be carried on stretchers. But it was high time to get away. The rainy season was approaching—this, in the Sudan, is called the winter, although it coincides with the astronomical summer. So for various reasons the journey had to be made but slowly.

There is no need to follow that return journey stage by stage. Though sometimes painful, it was none the less accomplished without serious incident or danger. Six weeks after leaving the ruins of Blackland, the column led by Captain Marcenay arrived at Timbuctoo. Two months later the heroes of this dramatic adventure disembarked in Europe, some of them in England and the others in France.

A few words will suffice to let the reader know what ultimately became of them.

To everyone his reward. M. Poncin rejoined his ministry and gave himself up, as of old, to the joys of statistics, continuing to discover, from time to time, something really "astounding." The average number of hairs among the world's different races, and the average growth of the human nail, by the year, by the month, by the hour, and by the second, at the various seasons, formed his most recent "finds."

So he is happy, for somewhere in the world he will always find something new to count. There is, however, one fly in his ointment; so far he has not been able to solve the problem set by Amédée Florence. But nothing here below is perfect.

Dr. Châtonnay has gone back into his professional harness and has got in touch with his patients, whose good health seemed hardly a compliment to him. Since he has become their physician all is again as it should be : they can afford the luxury of being ill, and just as they wish, but always to their own benefit, as it is by doctor's orders, they can come and go, or stay in bed or in their bedchamber.

M. le Député Barsac certainly "keeps to his chamber," but this is spelled with a capital C. Although the question of granting the vote to the negroes has been temporarily shelved, the overthrowing of the theory put forward by le Député du Midi has done no disservice to its author. It was evident, on the contrary, that the trials he had suffered, the risks he had run, deserved to be compensated. His position is thus firmer than ever before, and he is now being spoken of as the next Colonial Minister.

Malik and Tongané have left Africa. Following their mistress into England, they have got married. On British soil there now flourishes a charming little group of piccaninnies, of whom the first are already fairly big.

St. Bérain . . . but St. Bérain hasn't any history. He fishes and hunts, he still says "Madame" to people who wear moustaches and "Sir" to those of the opposite sex. Such are his main occupations. Otherwise, his history is identical with that of Jane Blazon; and, as hers is intimately associated with everything that concerns her brother Lewis and Captain Marcenay, the fate of all four can be indicated at once.

As might be expected, Marcenay, who as soon as he got to Timbuctoo asked for leave of absence—which this time was granted without demur—accompanied the three others to England.

During the month they had spent near the ruins of Blackland he had found leisure to describe, to the one who had now become his fiancée, the marvellous chance by which the message sent by Marcel Camaret arrived at its destination through the imponderable ether, the request he had made to Colonel

Allègre, and his distress when he was met by a categorical refusal.

Fortunately on the very next day, the reply had come from Colonel St. Auban. Not only did he declare that the order brought by the so-called Lieutenant Lacour was bogus, but he gave instructions that an expedition should at once be sent to the rescue of M. le Député Barsac, regarding whose fate he felt a very reasonable anxiety. Organized forthwith, the expedition set off down the Niger to Gao; and in crossing the desert beyond this point, Marcenay, who in spite of enormous difficulties was equipped with a field-gun, reached Blackland by a series of forced marches.

Scarcely had she arrived in England when Jane Blazon, with her brother, Captain Marcenay and St. Bérain, travelled by the quickest possible route to Glenor Castle, whence a telegram preceded them. Since she left it more than a year had elapsed. She now returned successful in her enterprise, the family honour restored to its original integrity.

In what condition would she find her father? Would the aged man, now ninety-four years old, have had the strength to endure his daughter's absence and to withstand the shame brought upon his second son by the robbery at the Central Bank? Certainly the press, after having done so much damage, had striven to repair it. Through the efforts of Amédée Florence, the moment he had got into touch with the outer world, they had proclaimed *urbi et orbi* the innocence of George and Lewis Blazon. But had the Lord of Glenor read the papers, or would this great happiness have reached him too late? Jane could not forget the condition her father had been in since the Central Bank business. Great as was her uneasiness, it was equalled by her anxiety to see him.

At last she arrived and was able to fall on her knees at the bedside of this aged man condemned to complete helplessness. Yet his eyes, alight with intelligence, showed that he still retained the clearness of his mind.

Accompanied by Lewis and St. Bérain as well as by Captain

Marcenay, whose presence she explained, the girl gave her father a complete account of her journey. She enumerated the witnesses to her narrative, and exhibited the attestation drawn up beside the grave at Koubo. She revealed something regarding which the press had so far kept silent, the hate which the wretched William Ferney had vowed towards the Blazon family and the dreadful methods by which he had satisfied it.

Everything held together. The Lord of Glenor could no longer doubt. Though one of his sons was dead, the honour of both had been saved.

The old man, his eyes fixed on his daughter, listened attentively. When she completed her narrative, a little blood reddened his face, his lips quivered, and his whole body trembled. His will was plainly struggling against the bonds which held his exhausted frame in their grip.

All who watched this tragic struggle were suddenly swept by an indescribable emotion. The will, stronger than the flesh, had triumphed. For the first time, after so many months, the Lord of Glenor was able to move. He could speak !

His transfigured face turned towards Jane; then, while his trembling hand sought that of the brave girl so deeply devoted to him, his lips murmured his thanks.

Then, as if at that very instant he had lost all reason for living, he gave a deep sigh, closed his eyes, and ceased to draw breath.

They strove in vain to revive him. Lord Blazon of Glenor had entered into his eternal rest as though he had fallen asleep. He was dead, but his end had been peace.

Here this story must end.

Of all its characters we now know the fate : Barsac, a future minister; M. Poncin, intoxicated with his statistics; Dr. Châtonnay, restored to his patients; St. Bérain, happy to be near his aunt-niece, and she happy to be Captain Marcenay's wife; Lewis Blazon, promoted to take charge of the Central Bank; Malik and Tongané, the parents of a thriving off-spring.

As for myself. . . .

Well, there! . . . There I'm prematurely disclosing the secret! . . . So let's say, as for Amédée Florence, he resumed his work with *L'Éxpansion Française,* in which he published the story of his adventures, which his editor valued at thirty centimes a line. To supplement his pay, the reporter, who was not a wealthy man, had the inspiration to kill two birds with one stone and to write a story on the same subject.

A story, you ask? . . . What story?

But it is the very one, dear readers, which, as you have reached these lines, you must have gone through from beginning to end.

A profound psychologist, Amédée Florence rightly thought that if he merely related the actual facts, he would make people yawn until they dislocated their jaws. Yet the same facts, told under the guise of fiction, might chance to give their readers a moment's entertainment. That's the way of the world. History, with a capital H, daunts us. Only stories amuse us . . . sometimes! What do you expect, we don't take things seriously nowadays!

These adventures being—unfortunately for himself—authentic, Amédée Florence has veiled his identity with a skill to which he must be the first to pay honour; by camouflaging them as fiction he hopes to make them go into a fair number of editions. This technique of proceeding from a newspaper article to notes jotted down from day to day and thence to an impersonal narrative, this method of exaggerating a somewhat audacious style and of going on to depict himself as a courageous and witty fellow, these little touches of spite, these little touches of flattery, all these bye-plots, these "dodges," these tricks of the trade, these literary artifices, may serve to hide more effectively the author's true identity.

But here he is at the end of his task. Good or bad, amusing or tedious, here is his book. So at last his incognito can be dropped without any repercussions, and his narrative can be revealed as authentic. And so its author, your most obedient and humble servant, can sign it with his own name—Amédée Florence, reporter to *L'Éxpansion Française*—before he writes those great words, those sublime words, that king of phrases :

THE END